DOGS AND (

BILJANA JOVANOVIĆ

DOGS
AND
OTHERS

Translated by John K. Cox

First published in 2018 by
Istros Books
London, United Kingdom www.istrosbooks.com

Copyright © Estate of Biljana Jovanović, 2018

This book was first printed in Serbia, *Psi i ostali* (Belgrade: Prosveta, 1980).

The right of Biljana Jovanović, to be identified as the author of this work has been
asserted in accordance with the Copyright, Designs and Patents Act, 1988

Translation © John K. Cox, 2018

Cover design and typesetting: Davor Pukljak, www.frontispis.hr

ISBN: 978-1-912545-16-2

The publisher wishes to acknowledge the support of
the Serbian Ministry of Culture & Media in the publication of this book.

Contents

Translator's Preface

Most names and other proper nouns in this translation have been left in their original Serbo-Croatian (as Jovanović would have said) forms. An exception was made for the most common version of the narrator's first name, Lidija, which we have rendered as Lidia for the sake of readability.

The text used as the basis for this translation was Biljana Jovanović's *Psi i ostali* (Belgrade: Prosveta, 1980).

Understanding This Book

Certain generalizations about plot or style, or specific notes on scenes, hard-won by another reader, can make a complex, or intricate, novel such as this one easier to understand. For instance, without a character list for the whole work, it might be helpful to untangle all the characters whose names begin with the letter 'M':

Marina – the mother of Lidia and Danilo, who is mostly absent and often cruel

Marko – Danilo's dodgy friend

Mihailo – the father of Lidia and Danilo, who hanged himself a decade or so ago

Milena – Lidia's lover, a friend of Danilo and Čeda Little River

Mira – Danilo's girlfriend

In terms of style, readers should be aware that Lidia's narration contains many meta-references (e.g., questions about things she just said) and 'experienced details' in the tradition of the French nouveau roman; there are also neologisms (sometimes adjectives, as in 'crumby', as opposed to 'crummy'; but often adverbs, as in 'postmanly' and 'bankerly-cordially') and, in recorded speech, drawled or drawn-out words spelled with urgently repeated vowels.

Subject matter such as bodily fluids (snot, semen, rheum, secretions connected to sexually-transmitted diseases), raw sexuality, and characters pinioned uncomfortably in the city's infernal machine might qualify the text as a kind of 'dirty realism', but its political content is equally obvious. The settling of accounts of a traditional-minded man (is it a man?) with. second-wave feminism in Chapter 25 is highly unsettling, but instructive.

There are many ways to read, or interpret, this novel. Literary critics have noted that it is here, in her second major work of prose, that Jovanović 'found her voice'. Indeed, her breakout success from two years earlier (1978), *Pada Avala* (Eng.: Avala is Falling) became a cult classic; and although it was, in the opinion of this translator, far too transgressive and energetic to deserve the label 'jeans prose', that is how it is often designated to this day. But *Dogs and Others* delivered a wholescale re-imagination of the role of the author and the narrator, and here Jovanović took her art to a different level. (Her third novel, *My Soul, My One and Only* from 1984, and her unfinished fourth novel from the 1990s, move into different territory yet again.)

Literary scholars, of course, also sort out how this book is put together, how it functions, and why it works. One notices immediately the pell-mell energy of the digressive narration; the intertextuality (various letters, pamphlets, and flashbacks set off

8

from the main text); the mystifying epigraphs; and the free and stubborn images – dreams looking for vocabulary, images looking for form. And yet, the novel holds together. The red threads lead somewhere. The references come home to roost. It's not a farce, not an ironic romp, not an act of heedless satire or feckless cynicism.

Consideration or analysis of the content of the novel is also both demanding and valuable. Jovanović herself noted that the novel was 'a debt, a debt to myself, to bring things that seemed important to me at the time out into the open, and to strip them completely naked'. Is this novel the fruit of the evolution of the increasing tide of creditable woman-centred writing in Yugoslavia, distilled into rocket fuel by the addition of feminist sensibilities from the West? How important is the fact that this novel contains what appears to be the first detailed depiction of a sexual relationship between two women in Serbian literature?

Interesting historical explanations, stressing the socio-economic or even political context of the plot and the times in which the manuscript was produced and published, are also possible. Jovanović was too young to be a direct part of the 'generation of 1968', but not too young to engage or interact (positively and negatively) with that movement's causes and ideals. She was definitely too young to be considered one of the 'children of communism'. Related phenomena such as membership in the 'red bourgeoisie' or, as some of her critics might say, her generation's position as beneficiaries of post-war social mobility who supposedly repaid the system with unruliness or anarchism also miss the mark, but they are in circulation. Also plausible are critiques of work like hers from the Marxist or neo-Marxist; the presence of the *Praxis* philosophers in Yugoslavia during her lifetime provides a lot of ready material for analysis. One could also take, ideologically or historically, a Titoist perspective, whereby Jovanović's novels can be seen to deviate from the established canon of 'socialist aestheticism' or 'Partisan realism'. One could also maintain, as does this observer, that Jovanović's attention to radically new subjects and her transgressive literary innovations amount to social criticism, which in turn represents a kind of urban extension, and logical continuation, of the 'anti-fascist moment' of World War II.

John K. Cox, Fargo, USA. 2018

*

This translation is dedicated to William E. 'Bill' Schmickle, the most brilliant teacher I ever had. No one ever lit up Founders Hall or Duke Memorial with ideas and lectures and writing the way he did, and no professor ever pushed me as hard or rewarded me as generously.

BILJANA JOVANOVIĆ

DOGS AND OTHERS

In Place of an Introduction

This story does not consist of night-and-day phantasmagorias, but of Dogs and Others. No joke: Others and Dogs. Since a position favouring the relativity of truth is psychologically more justifiable than one favouring the absoluteness of truth, and since it's not out of the question that it's also epistemologically more reliable, then it's true – and let us thank God for it – it's true, that which is written in books, in church and in other places: Dogs always believe that they belong to Others (whom they consider to be, for unknown reasons enduring right up to our day, better than they are). The Others are not always convinced that they are not themselves Dogs. Still, though, Dogs are Others and Others are Dogs. The one thing that actually distinguishes them from each other, now and again (and something that justifies singling them out for participation in this story), is the level of their (as numerous personages are wont to say, and learned ones at that) social adaptation.

What nonsense! What's this sort of thing supposed to mean to Dogs? Or especially to Others?

Whatever – both the one group and the other suffocate in the same typical stinking mess that is life:

I

For a longish, and rounded, amount of time (like a lie on Jaglika's lips), I took, with the certainty of an idiot, her stories and those of Marina to be images from my own childhood; and of course I believed unshakably in my ownership of those images. I'm not sure when that all went up in smoke! All efforts up to this point have been inaudible (unsuccessful), like clacking one's dry, untrimmed fingernails together or timidly scratching the edge of a table with a pin; there was a huge tangle in my head and I felt it whenever I tried to remember something, or with inappropriate ambition tried to recall anything at all with complete accuracy; the bit that I could get my hands on was quickly lost amid the concentric braid of other pictures, and there was no way for me to find the beginning or the end. And then everything snapped, went off like a bomb; no; like a hundred and twenty glasses tossed from the tenth floor; and nothing remained; not even anything like the rubber stub that's left behind when a balloon pops or, you know, an inflated plastic bag explodes.

I was free! I realized that I remembered nothing, that, instead of me, Jaglika and Marina were doing the remembering; that I had never recalled anything; and that the two of them were swindling me and, sneakily, and stealthily (kisses and baby-talk), pulling me into the mutual family memory. I thought: such gratitude for emptiness! I could shove everything inside (where it's empty, like into the biggest hole in the world); falsehoods from anybody; even the most far-fetched, random fabrications. That's how I started off inventing my own childhood; with no malice and no vanity; with empty space inside myself, around me, all around, everywhere…

Everything that I would think up and narrate to myself, in a whisper at first; once or twice – depending on the length of the story; and then I would repeat it out loud, before going to sleep, with my eyes wide open, in the dark; and the story (an image from childhood – which only appeared not to exist) would settle into its spot in my brain.

The next day I checked: I would sneak up on Jaglika, and start up a conversation first about her glasses, then her aching joints, homeless women and cuckolded men; and then, in the middle of the conversation, I would say, as if by chance: 'Hey, *baba*, do you remember that?' Or: 'What was that like, *baba*? You used to know that… ' Jaglika would ask what I was getting at, and wriggle joyously in her seat – happy that I had faith in her memory, and that's how she fell into the trap. I told her only the basic framework of a story (the picture), devised the night before, leaving out the dates and more detailed parts; otherwise Jaglika would discover my deception. And so she could continue the stories one after another to the end.

For several days running, I carried every fabricated story (in my arms, in my mouth) to the half-deaf and half-blind Jaglika. The fact that Jaglika took part wholeheartedly in it all only showed that it was realistic to assume that all the pictures (stories), from this point on, as far as the eye could see, all of them made or invented by night, happened or were happening, or were just about to happen, at some time or other and to some person or other, or even to me!

At that point it took me a great deal of time to realize that I imagined some of these things as: freedom of fabrication, that is to say, freedom of memory; one could say that I was suffering from unknown illnesses, but I had attributed special significance to them; I thought I'd be able to disconnect from the family memory (Jaglika the creator – her memories go back the furthest; Marina the great magus; Danilo and I, the assistants; our relatives – probationary helpers) simply because I truly recalled nothing! And that the flexible hole (no limits) in my brain was the reason that I believe I became a heretic by my own volition and merit; and in fact every invention was overloaded in advance; it was only possible to concoct things according to how they happened and not in any other way. And it all looked like this: I'd think up a story; I'd try absolutely as hard as I could (dear God, it's so taxing!) not to alter it even the tiniest bit; I'd push it (the story), just temporarily; I'd move it around exactly as much as necessary for space to open up, at least one tiny little spot in my otherwise meagrely-stocked brain, for the next image (story); and so on, one after the other; I'd find a spot for one, and when the next one arrived, I'd move it, and when the third one came in, I'd even have to squish that second one, too; but before I'd compress it I'd push it gently and politely to the back, as if we were on the bus: 'Just a bit more, if you don't mind, so I can set down my bag… Beg your pardon, oh little brain of mine with the images, make a little room for me!' And then they (the ones in the bus) would say: 'Check that out. As if her pictures, or her brain, were anything special. I mean, really!'

To tell the truth, there is one little thing pertaining to the fabrication of childhood that turns out to be an advantage when compared to a non-fabricated, so-called genuine childhood: there isn't any subconscious or similar understory; there's no interpretation; there is none of that clowning around with psychoanalysis; the possible objection from those quarters (from the psychoanalysts and other, different people) would call into question completely my invention of a childhood (calling it non-memory, or the equivalent thereof) – such a thing (my thing) simply isn't possible all by itself; that it would come down like a bolt out of the blue without reasons, up there in the blue; but since psychoanalysis still cannot discern how something started, and that is its position, at least as far as I'm concerned – at the bottom of the water with a stone on my neck, plus a rope – but for others, okay, maybe it's not quite drowning but it is 'That's kind of like old news, or a little bit pregnant.'

So what I told Jaglika went like this: there were dark hallways all around me; on the walls hung small black and white pictures of various animals, like those little drawings in the chocolate bars that came in the blue wrappers; these extremely tall people kept showing up; more and more of them; I think it was always at noon (how did I know that, if there wasn't any window!); they measured my forehead; they wrote on some pieces of paper; shook their heads as they were leaving, every one of them did it and they all did it the same way (as if they were duplicates, or rather doubles, of each other) and always, I mean really every time, they said the same thing: 'Her face is narrow and ill-humoured; see you tomorrow, goodbye!'

And Jaglika told it to me like this: 'The dark corridors are the basement where we used to live; it was always dark; you were sick with scarlet fever; that's when Dr Vlada used to come by, every single day … Do you remember Vlada? … He checked in on you … You weren't good for anything, and we all thought you were going to die …'

Thus, according to Jaglika, the little pictures on the walls were flypaper strips, and the pieces of paper were prescriptions; since it was dark, the fact that it seemed like midday to me was the result of a large high-wattage lamp, which Dr Vlada would turn on above my head, and so forth.

Fantastic! Jaglika thought it all up; indeed Jaglika did think it all up, as did I, incidentally! Never, and I knew this for sure, never did we live in a basement; we never had sticky fly-paper tape on our walls; and especially never any lamp with a big bright bulb; I never had scarlet fever, and so on… After several similar attempts (a tale told to Jaglika; with her just fabricating it differently) I was no longer capable of differentiating what was Jaglika's from what was mine from what was a third party's, that Jaglika, as demiurge, truly remembered (the right of the creator is untouchable even when she is lying). It seemed to me that I was again getting tangled in a snare (what a stupid animal!) of other people's memories, no matter whether real or fabricated, and that the imagined freedom of emptiness has the shape and the sizzle of a lie, a lie from Jaglika's cracked lips. I gave up on talking to anyone, save to myself, in the evening, in the dark, eyes wide open; along with all the others, I received a new power of imagination: I believed that every story was irrevocably true.

But Jaglika did not leave off; she enjoyed talking and watching my face full of trust (a creator also needs flattery); she extracted from her head piece after piece of outright lying (truly one never knows!), carefully, as if she were brushing lock after lock of her hair, which by the way did not exist; I did not have many opportunities, more precisely, I had just one possibility: '*Baba*, how about if I read the newspaper out loud. Eh, granny? Put those stories of yours away for now!' Jaglika, however, would shake her head unhappily, bring her morning cup (full of dust – it was already noon) of tea (the orator was taking refreshment) to her lips and go on babbling;

she just pushed those little extracts right into my ears, along with her lies, which were no worse than mine but for exactly that reason created unbearable confusion in my head. '*Baba*, stop it … That's not important anymore, it's the past,' I said repeatedly; and then I would cover her in loud headlines from her favourite newspapers: *woman is the pillar of the family, woman factory owner kills her child so her lover will marry her, directions for large and small needlepoint projects, freshen up your surroundings;* and in this way, not stopping until I was dead certain that Jaglika had forgotten what she'd been recalling; and until she stopped grumbling: 'OK, OK, but I've got a good one for you.' Normally this took half an hour, sometimes less, and then Jaglika's face would light up; then I would wander around the room looking for her glasses – she never knew where she'd left them just a moment before, but they were always either on the window sill or under her pillow.

II

A famous Yugoslav poet, a woman, well known in those days, in my house, in my room, while Danilo and Jaglika were sleeping; she had hung her polyester panties on the highest hook on my clothes-tree; she lifted her skirt part-way up (exposing her huge flabby thighs) and headed off to the bathroom; her lover lay on my bed, a man twenty years younger than she was, and hence a little older than me, with a low brow, a conspicuously low brow, and with long, bowed legs (that's all I was able to see since the rest of his serviceable body remained under the blanket); the poet hadn't shut the door, neither the one to the bedroom nor the one to the bathroom, and thus Danilo, who, judging from everything, hadn't slept a wink since the two of them had entered the house, found her bent over the sink, with her legs spread (maybe under the sink!). There he stood, thunderstruck, and then he sprinted into his room, embarrassed, frightened; he stared at me, goggle-eyed (I was seated on the floor) and at the poet's lover on the bed, and then back at me, and slamming his door shut, he ran into his room without uttering a word, not even one letter of a word, not even a sound, without anything really (God, it was as if he'd been struck dumb by horror). In a little while the poet came by with her hitched-up skirt, asking for a towel.

That night I slept in Jaglika's room, on a mattress; on the floor; right up till morning I listened to Jaglika's diligent snoring, whimpering, and the grinding of her teeth. I was convinced that all this wasn't coming out of her toothless mouth. Instead, the noises were souls, the souls of her Montenegrin-Hungarian ancestors, which, like all species of Hymenoptera, obdurately, annoyingly, the whole blessed night (the lamp on the table near the head of her bed was turned on – Jaglika was afraid to dream in the dark, and incidentally so am I) flew circles around her head, and from time to time around mine, probably remembering that I am Jaglika's descendant. In view of the fact that my grandmother, with her Hymenoptera, the lamp she left on, the quinces beneath the radiator, the sputum in the old newspapers four thick under her bed, was in the other part of the apartment, I couldn't hear Danilo's creeping about or his pacing, clearing his throat occasionally (like the kind in movies about fear and terror) in front of the door to the room in which the poet and her lover were sleeping. They were going to tell me all that the next day. Among other things, that Danilo at least ten times during the night (so the poetess said, but poets, male and female, love to exaggerate of course) opened their door all the way and just stood there, every time, in the door-frame, immobile, for several minutes (that's what the poet said: several minutes) and, she said, for that reason the two of them couldn't sleep a wink. At first they called out to him to come in, they turned on the light; the poet said she had not seen such a beautiful and spectral boy for ages; I told her that he would be twenty-nine this fall and that he wasn't a boy, but she reiterated: 'The little guy stared with those enormous eyes of his and he stood there, just stood there so awkwardly!' Danilo does have bulging eyes, but otherwise, cross my heart, and cross something lower if I have to, there were a lot of things about this that mattered to her, but that doesn't matter.

That day they left at noon; the lover rubbed his watery eyes, offering me at the same instant his other hand, small and perspiring, but warm; the poet was visibly angry, and she didn't say goodbye, but Danilo said, from the doorway when the two of them were in the lift, happily, serenely, like he was hitting a ping-pong ball their way: 'Why didn't you go to a hotel? It definitely would have been more to your liking there!'

But then, in the very next minute, I hear the poet's voice from the street: 'Lidiaaa! Lidiaaa!' I ran down the stairs (I could have broken both of my legs). There was Danilo, dear God he was down there, how'd that happen so fast, just a moment ago he … .

He was standing there clinging to her chubby upper arm like a little child as he said over and over, stuttering, with spittle on his lips and an incomprehensible plea in his bulging eyes: 'Why don't you come by for a visit… Why don't you drop in… ' and then, catching sight of me: 'Lida, tell them, tell her, Lida… ' The poet smiled, a touch maliciously and a little bit like a bad actress; the lover stared at Danilo like at a rabid (dangerous) but pathetic dog.

All that day Danilo kept on asking me, at short intervals, 'Why didn't you tell them? Why didn't you say it, Lida?' Not completely certain of myself, and pretty much exhausted, I replied that the poet and her lover had just left, a moment ago, or two hours ago, but for Christ's sake really recently, and what could he want now, anyway, he had walked them out, he had seen them off all nice and proper, the poet and the lover with the officer's cap pulled all the way down over his low forehead, and now they've probably gone to a hotel, or on to another city; 'For God's sake, Danilo, you told them to do that yourself!'

That's when Danilo's feelings of abandonment started to grow: he ran after unknown people in the street, he turned people back as they left our building, he called out to them from the window, beseeching them, making them swear, acting like a cry-baby to get them to return, to drop in on us; and all of them save Marko (Danilo's friend from senior and primary school) shook their heads (as if they were sages), swaggered about and thought and stared the same way the poet and her lover did: this boy is ill (pathetic dog), this boy is dangerous (mad dog), and they stopped coming by. He asked the taxi driver who drove us to Mira's place (she was Danilo's pretend girlfriend) whether he loved him, to which the taxi driver wisely replied that he basically didn't have any reason to hate him, and that for him Danilo was a customer just like any other customer. Danilo insisted that the man come up with an answer about loving him or not, which was for heaven's sake nothing if not appropriate, since the question had been whether he loved him or not, and not whether he had a reason to hate him. Later, when we had arrived (after a few minutes), as I was rummaging about in my purse looking for money, Danilo said to the taxi driver: 'I should introduce you two. This is my sister Lidia.'

He locked himself in his room for days and nights on end. He didn't go out, at least during the time I was at home. Jaglika, near the end of her days and on the verge of dying, with thoughts and memories that were twenty years old, or fifty, and then twenty again, asked: 'Where has my Dankitsa gotten to? I haven't seen him since he was only this big, you know?'

And then came a switch: for the whole day, when I was off at the library, he sat with Jaglika; and when I came home he didn't budge from my side, until late in the evening – he'd fall asleep in my bed with his head squeezed up against my back. In the morning he'd be awake before me, and a long while before Jaglika would start to shout from the other side of the house: 'Lidiaaa!'

As if he hadn't slept at all, his eyes were opaque and yet again, too big, prominent.

'In which bedroom can I take cover?'

'Huh? Danilo, you're in a bedroom.'

'You don't get it at all … Anyway. What room do I go to? Don't play the fool here.'

'Danilo, I'm in a rush to get to work. Go to sleep.'

'But really, Lidiaaa … I'm asking you. What's wrong with that fat old bag-lady in there?'

'What are you ranting about? What fat lady?'

'Don't even pretend like you don't know, Lidia!'

'Listen, Danilo, I'm gonna be late for work.'

'You're always urging me to love people but I can't love them and that fat woman can't do it either, just so you know. Not even grandma can stand it anymore, in case you were wondering.'

'I'm in a hurry, Danilo. Good grief. I've got no time.'

'Why are you shouting, why are you always shouting, Lidia?'

'Put a sock in it, you idiot. Go see what Jaglika's doing! Off you go now.'

'Hold on, Lidia. I told you, and *Baba* will tell you, that she's not going to put up with that naked fool any more, just so you know. You're always dragging them into the house and nobody can stand it any more. And by the way that woman's a whore.'

'Stop it you jerk that's enough!'

'Why are you screaming … Why are you screaming?!'

'Go check on what grandma's up to … ' and with that I slammed the door behind me; Danilo's yells followed me to the front door of the building, and as I was running across the street, I could hear him, probably from the balcony now (I didn't turn around) as he roared and cursed.

III

'There will never exist a person who possesses definite knowledge of the gods and of the matters I am talking about. And even if this person were in a position to tell the whole truth, he or she would know that this wasn't the case. But all people get to have their own imagination.'
– (R.P. Lo4 [X of K.] J.B.)

'Hey listen, Lidia, last night I had another dream about that riot of colours; first they ran, and then they jostled each other, golden yellow, purplish green and stale wine-red, and dark red, too, and that beige like Mira's skirt, and a blue, a thin blue colour, you know the one, Lida, it always whizzes by like lightning, my head starts aching from it, it's like a whistle, Lida, it whizzes and flashes and then goes boom – that's all she wrote – Lida, are you listening to me?'

I nod my head and think to myself how dead certain I am that Danilo is devouring at least two bars of chocolate at the same time when he chomps and spits so unbearably like this, with saliva running from the corners of his mouth. I go on picking up the newspapers strewn about and say to him: 'I'm listening to you. Go on!' And he says: 'I dreamt that Mira came, with an enormous towel around her head, as if she'd been washing her hair, and all at once everything on her started to drip, like an ice cream cone, just like that, Lidia... Then, behind her, there appeared that guy from a few days ago, the guy with the three sweaters on, d'you hear,

Lidia, the guy who slept with that naked fat creature, the one that Grandma said she couldn't stand to see any more, and she came, too, only I didn't see her right away; it was only after Mira and the guy got undressed and lay down on that towel from her head; it was like they were cadavers, Lidia, they just lay there and didn't move any more; and Mira, she was hideously thin … then I saw that fat, naked lady; actually, she came up to me from behind and plugged my ears with some pinkish plugs, terribly hard, and she started rubbing me here, behind my earlobes and then eventually my eyelids, Lida, just imagine that. She was so rude, Lidia! Lidia, is she always so rude? When she started to undress me, it was so unbalanced, by that I mean all from her side, as if she'd gone bonkers, she was shaking all over – she broke the belt loop on my pants and Lidia the moment she touched my zip I went half-crazy and when she unbuttoned me down there I came like a rifle, all over her, Lida, I splattered her everywhere, and she just seemed lost in thought, she pretended that she didn't see. Afterwards that beige colour spread over us, beige darkness, you understand? Nothing was visible for a while, like looking through watery sand, right up until the pent-up colour came hissing out of Mira's eyes, with interruptions, like when you pee and have an irregular stream, very similar … Afterwards I saw that you were standing off to one side and you were, like this, look, Lida, on your middle finger like this you were spinning a pair of nail scissors and behind you Jaglika was hopping around, whispering something to you, and then came the worst part with the colours, Lida, are you listening to me … and Lida, stop that now, stop it, Lida, sit down …'

Danilo wasn't actually munching on any chocolate, but he did, however, have something in his mouth, and that's why he was talking so slowly; and an enormous lie was rolling around on his palate, between his teeth, and burst forth from under his tongue, Danilo's speech was unintelligible, Danilo was lying, sizzlingly, spraying on all sides like Jaglika – who ever since that day was no longer able to walk, as if her legs had been hit by a thunderbolt (Jaglika, sweet Jaglika, she knows that the devil himself had sent some invisible boulders rolling down, and that's why she couldn't move), or perhaps that blue colour that Danilo never ceases dreaming about, the blue thin one, flashes, goes bang and that's all she wrote … But all of it together, a phantasmagoria in Svetosavska Street. Danilo and Jaglika, the heroes of a cartoon in fiery blue, with a devil who bombards people with stones, and with Mira's ice-cream tan skirt.

'Danilo, it looks like you've become unhinged.' He was looking at me with a crooked smile, like a crook (am I imagining this?), but the very next moment, with his eyes half-closed from fear (I could see quite well the tiny white particles of rheum in between his eyelashes) and with his head turned aside just a touch – out of fright – it was as if I was holding a whip in my hands, and not his moist smelly shirt. I yelled: 'You told my dream … my dream – and you distorted it completely, you idiot. Idiiiot … You made up half of it … My dream, you animaaal!' But Danilo wasn't scared any more (that was also my imagination) but rather dejected and embarrassed, Danilo the five-year-old boy, Jaglika's most beloved little grandson, using this for a moment to garner all the security he could – from the very fact that everybody else loved him more than me, and that all of them (all of whom?) at that moment were standing at his back and with composure, and a taunt of sorts, he says, 'But Lida, calm down! Everybody all around can hear. I had that dream, I dreamt it last night, Lida, calm down, I beg you … Just drop it … Lida, really, I …'

I'd had enough: I ripped his shirt; once more he gave me such a weird look that I didn't know what was going on ... that thing with his eyes (he's cross-eyed) or something else connected with the ripped shirt, or with my wrath, or because he knew ... he was looking at me like that because he knew that I had related that dream recently, but of course Danilo also knew that I'd told that dream only to him.

After the torn shirt, it was his leg's turn, and his head's and shoulder's, anything, I wanted to hit him ... But all I did was kick him, not all that hard, no, definitely not hard enough to make him scream and call out for Jaglika; then I pulled him by his hair and when I truly was about to hit him (no, I did want to kill him: in my hand was a heavy, sharp object, one without a blade), he turned around so contorted, and twisted (scoliosis?), pulled away, and ran off to Jaglika – in the direction of her omnipotent lap – as if she could help him!

Anyway, Jaglika couldn't see how the dreams meant anything to her, dreams were just omens, indicators of the events of future days; at night she dreamt and in the daytime it came true, at least a little bit, at least in part – and that was sufficient – that was enough for her; all the rest was frightful stupidity that only silly people messed with: Danilo and I. Poor Jaglika wasn't going to get it even after she was dead; she was never going to get this dream thing. Even if a hundred of her Hymenopterae started work on convincing her, whispering into her bulbous ears – covered in little curly grey locks of her already faded hair, even if I do say so, one hundred souls of her ancestors would gather and like one terribly complicated tribe – forgetting the quarrels and discord that belong to time – for they are hymenopterous timeless beings

(Jaglika did not allow an insect of any kind to be killed in her room, in fact, not even a flying one) and started enthusiastically to persuade her to put dreams aside – someplace where there's room for them so that she does not touch them, or interpret them, so that she doesn't conceive of them by any means (not for anything in the world) as theirs or anyone else's and especially not divine messages; Jaglika would make fun of them, dismiss us with a wave of her hand, laugh at them again, rub her right eye and her left eye (the lid) and again, my God, again she'd laugh at them… and then it could happen that she would say: 'I know more about dreams than all of you over there from that gang that gets together and dreams about everything and does nothing else, and afterwards you hold court and talk and then go and dream some more and on and on, again and again… I know more, more about dreams.'

'Jaglika, when you're dreaming, do you know it's a dream; do you know while you're asleep that you are dreaming?' – I asked her, very much anticipating that she would betray some secret to me, or something very much like a secret. But Jaglika gave me a look like the Devil himself (her power over me was the certainty of an animal, the neighbour's dog, let's say, when it is squatting to piss – the way Jaglika does, by the way – the dog is a female, and for me, as for all wretches, there's nothing left to do but amass and harbour hatred towards dogs and Jaglika) and she said, 'Oh, you miserable girl, and I thought you were smarter than that.'

If I didn't know that I was dreaming when I'm dreaming, I could with total presence of mind state that dreams were definite, in the way that reality is; that they are a parallel world and how it's in point of fact my personal dichotomy (in the back, by the occipital bone); I could even rejoice at the lack of necessity of subsequent connection, of the subordination of dreams to reality or of reality to dreams, which is actually what Jaglika and the whole world do, or the whole world and Jaglika: what harmony! The whole difficulty, however, lies in the fact that, when I dream, that's when I have some half-retarded control that constantly warns me that I'm dreaming, I'm only dreaming, and then, thank God, all the knives, the awls, the daggers with their sundry grips and all their various blades sticking in my neck and my fingers and face, and more often in strangers' faces and in everybody's backs and everyone's eyes – they look like plastic children's toys, bendable and soft and harmless; but they aren't, they are not that at all; and at any rate I have no control like that (no distance from my own self) when I'm not dreaming; and so, thanks to the terrible disproportionality between sleep and so-called wakefulness (or whatever other names that marvel goes by) and a little indirect mediation here and a little direct intervention there, I am in a double trap, and that worries Jaglika, my mother Madame Marina, and Marina's husband: they would all say, flat out and one after the other, and rightly so, with complete rectitude and perfect indifference: 'It's all your own fault,' like that time twenty-five years ago or more when for the first time I ruined a pair of newly purchased shoes (Marina maintained that I'd deliberately spent the entire morning standing in a puddle: 'This is all your fault. You're not getting any new ones.' I wore wet shoes that whole semester – I absolutely could not get them to dry out. But no – I wore an old pair, all ripped up.

And Danilo? Danilo takes my dreams, he lies and he steals, and he stays silent about his own dreams, not a word, not a syllable, but nothing and utterly nothing; only occasionally, when he is with Jaglika, does he whisper something. Danilo is my informer; he rats my dreams out to me, and rats me out to Jaglika. Could it be that Danilo simply has no dreams? He does not even sleepwalk, although that's a most ordinary, trivial thing; but consequently he peers through the lock into my room while I'm sleeping (he's been awake for several years running) and he steals what I'm dreaming about, and later he tells it to Jaglika, but only to her, fortunately.

A Picture from Childhood

Marina took Danilo and me to Tivoli one time! She arranged my left hand across Danilo's right, squeezed our fingers (safety snaps), and then she checked the buttons on our identical coats, turned up our collars – she thought (at the time) that the wind was blowing but in fact it wasn't (I know it wasn't); she ran her hand quickly, impatiently, across our heads (the backs of two identical heads) and, as always, both Danilo and I felt the electricity popping from her palm. I thought (at the time) that faces were distorted and became half-shy or half-perverted grins – creditable grins, like masks at New Year's – all because of this little current from Marina's palm; but it wasn't like that, it wasn't that; Marina knows that it wasn't because of that. Then she told us: 'Go walk around a bit!' For the first few moments, while she was still right behind our backs (like a policeman on the beat – the parent's burden) and our identical itsy-bitsy smoothed-down heads, we walked along (three or four or five steps) like we were glued together – so we'd make the right impression on Marina, and then we both set off running without letting go of each other's hands and we soon fell down. Danilo hurt his chin and scraped both of his arms (his coat tore), and it was probably the exact same for me. Okay, maybe it wasn't his arms or shoulders, but his knees, it's quite likely that it was his knees, but I can't rule out that the scrapes and scratches were everywhere – on all the hard parts of his body. From that point on, the weird things started happening: whenever Marina would take us to the park, the woods, or for a ride on the merry-go-round, Danilo and I, although our hands were not hooked together, walked pressed up against one another and when we'd start to run, always, the same thing always happened, the same strange thing: it was as if we tripped each other up but no one else saw it, no one else could see it, and we would crash into each other. Then Marina, practical and wise (indifferent), when we had in the course of just one spring ruined all our trousers and jumpers, decided to keep us far apart from each other; at first, when she took us to the park or the woods or anywhere like that, she put herself in the middle, in between us (my God, it was meters of distance… let's say, without exaggerating, it was two full meters), with me on the left side and Danilo on her right. When we came back it was vice-versa, Danilo on her left side and me on the right. In the lift it was one of us in front (underneath, with your head below her large maternal bosom) and the other in back, with your head at the level of her waist. Indeed, in the lift there was truly no chance (or only a negligible one) for activity that would result in torn clothing, but Marina, being practical and enterprising (those two things go together) and, a third thing, too – efficient, careful (those are one and the same) – considered precautionary measures everywhere at any time and in any place (great or small) to be indispensable, even though it might strike a person (a figure) on the outside as silly and superfluous.

IV

Jaglika has stopped walking; of course I didn't doubt that Satan himself had knocked nails into her from her hips down; in all truth. I was forced to call up Marina, our household god, who always knows everything – especially when it's a matter of missing leg-power, doctors, cemetery clerks, politicians, connections, and money. And so, Madame Marina telegraphed this in response to the long and totally helpless letter that Danilo and I wrote: 'Find someone, will send money!' That was it. What divine simplicity and efficiency! But even gods, especially household ones, have been to known to fly off the handle (the divine head through a wall of plaster) if they haven't thought things through thoroughly: a couple of days after the first telegram, a second one followed, completely Epimetheus-like, and even sympathetic: 'I will pay half the costs and Lidia half love you all mama stop.' Whatever else she was (and she was a lot of other things) the household god was a skinflint, a miser, a tightwad, a piece of shit, a scum-bag. I believe that my life would have been five thousand times easier if Madame Marina had already just gone ahead and died there in Milan, of a severe (once and for all) heart attack (from which there's no return) and emancipated me (sweet Jesus!) from her efficiency, her villainous *joie de vivre*, her money, and other stupid shit like that. Efficient people, regardless of whether they have political power or that of a prostitute, and that's six of one and half a dozen of the other, are the lowest wretches that tread on the surface of this earth, many, many times more miserable than those miscreants who dream of this power, who desire it. And then (if my mother died from that severe attack of her heart), I would telegraph to Marina's husband there in Milan: 'send money for funeral stop' or, for example: 'I will pay half and you half, down payment necessary, cemetery admin does not work for free, expenses for transport for you to pay, stop.' But I know, I know very well, that my mother's husband would read this telegram with a scornful grin, one of these two completely hypothetical telegrams, and he'd see everything through to completion himself, and then afterwards make conspiratorial comments along the lines of 'the daughter takes after her mother that way.'

I ran an advertisement in all of the existing city newspapers; I inquired of several people whether they knew of some fool who would, for minimal pay drive, walk, and clean up after a hundred-year-old creature who is worn out but eager to live. Naturally enough no one answered the ad. Danilo began to panic: he searched, he turned the whole house upside down, removed all the drawers, shoved all the boxes out of sight, to find the non-existent addresses of non-existent relatives. Then a guy turned up, Čeda of Rečica (Little River). He nodded his head, kept saying 'No sweat', addressed me as '*Miiisss*' and called Danilo 'the young fellow'; but he was the sweetest of all to Jaglika (but good Lord, there's no comparison to the sweetness of the sales clerk downstairs in the grocery store): 'How is the lady of the house *todaaay*?' (He always drew out the last word, and the penultimate one, too) … 'How's granny *doooing*?'

As soon as they got to know each other, Jaglika told Čeda from Little River that all women are whores, especially those who don't look like it, and that he should be careful, and watch his back. Čeda nodded his head, rubbed his palms together, and exited Jaglika's room without saying a word. Later, pretending to be a trouble-maker, he said to Danilo, 'She's a dragon-lady, that one.'

He came three times a week, always right at the agreed time; this Čeda the Flow got on my nerves. He'd wait and give indulgent little laughs, sweating, his shoulders always hunched over, while I combed out Jaglika's five hairs, put on her shoes, searched for her scarf, glasses or purse. And on it went like that, exactly, for a month; the little ring at the door, Čeda's hunched shoulders, a smile like posing for a police photographer, Jaglika's shoes, her coat or her glasses, whatever. On the same day that he'd done everything for the short, fat (if only in her legs) and spoiled Jaglika and then left (he always hunkered over her, with his shoulders hunched up), he would also call up on the telephone after an hour or two and say: 'Miss *Lidiaaa*, know what I forgot to tell you? Our charge had three servings of apricot juice today, and she went to the bathroom twice, and afterwards, you know, she forgot and left her glasses in Košutnjak where we had been, and I had to go back. That's going to be more petrol for you all ...'

And so Čeda of Little River demanded, received, calculated, thanked, hunched his shoulders, retracted his head, and repeated pointlessly: 'No problem whatever you say Miss Lidia, everything is just fine, *goodbyyye.*'

Then he disappeared; he wasn't around for an entire week; Jaglika complained to Danilo about the dirty house, the closed windows, the hideous food, poison in the coffee, and how she was strong and would somehow manage to survive it all, I mean the poison and the stuffy air and the stink and all the other non-sense – 'and whatever else occurs to that no-goodnik of a girl'. She convinced Danilo that I drove off 'that fine upstanding boy'; so that once Danilo actually came up to me and asked, in earnest (it was just after I'd woken up), if I'd hooked up with Čeda the Flow – '*Baba* says guaranteed you attacked him'; she told him that I wanted, I really really wanted, to pluck that drawn-in head off his shoulders and then pluck out whatever else on him was drawn in. Danilo, who was naturally unconvinced that my hands were clean in the matter of Čeda's disappearance (how had Jaglika turned him?) kept on asking me, the whole blasted morning: 'But tell me, Lidia… Do you hear me Lidia – how come you won't tell me?!'

A Picture from Childhood

I'd just come back from school; I remember that period for two significant things: I was unfathomably small in stature and I had the skinniest legs of anyone on our street, or in the whole school; Marina was actually honestly afraid that my legs would break, and she took me to twenty doctors and told me to be careful how I walked, and not to run at all. As for my growth, that was simply fantastical, like the little girl in this or that fairy tale, and I was the smallest girl in the entire city, and perhaps in the whole country – there aren't, you know, any stats about height, the average height of children in those days, but I do know that in the fourth grade I still looked like I was in kindergarten. So here's how I conceived of this story from childhood: I came home from school and found no one at home; I didn't have a key; they never gave me a key – everyone in the house (and this included Marina's pestilent dog) was afraid of bandits, informers, thieves, and other marvels – and, thinking that a key, once fallen from Danilo's or my satchel, would surely, instantaneously be found by someone who would destroy us, kill us, rob us blind, Jaglika and Marina used to make us wait for hours out in front of our building. The other children carried keys knotted onto string, and their mothers put the string around their children's necks or around their wrists, but most often around their waists. Marina shook her head and said, 'That can be broken in a heartbeat and then ... that's all she wrote' – whenever I demanded a key from her and a string to go around my neck or wrist. Her utterance 'that's all she wrote' was unadulterated magic: in the same second I would imagine a whole horde of brutal people who thanks to my key (the broken string) broke into our home, smashing windows, the door, the dressers, beating Marina, Jaglika and Danilo, kicking the dog (I, of course, was spared, and none of these people touched me, and it even seems to me now that one of those imaginary guys gave me a wink, back then). Later I'd imagine how the neighbours would carry out a completely dead Marina, a battered and thrashed Jaglika, and Danilo, with a broken leg. And so out of fear of Marina, and not of these imaginary images, I utterly stopped asking for a key and a string. I waited more times than I could count in front the door; there was one time when it was terribly long, and I didn't know what to do, and I felt like an entire day had passed without anyone turning up. I walked back and forth, around in a circle, back and forth again, with my hands deep in my pockets. I was trying my hardest to punch through my pockets (I was angry and totally powerless); sometimes I cried, most likely, like a superstitious grownup would do, because of Marina's 'that's all she wrote', and I rode the lift up and down thinking that one of them, and it would be Jaglika, had already shown up and was now hiding in the dark. She didn't turn on the light in the apartment, so I couldn't see her from the street and she was doing that on purpose because I bore a resemblance to my father, and she simply could not abide him, and she was constantly, constantly saying that she knew only one complete idiot on this planet, and she'd cross herself and thank the Lord that he was no longer with us. At that age I didn't win any prizes for outstanding intelligence; I even looked a bit stupid – and I was, for instance, convinced that there were at least five entrances to our building, but only two actually existed – one off the court-yard and one from the street, but the one through the courtyard was, in addition, seldom unlocked. Such hesitations and similar bagatelles were readily visible on my face. It seemed that I, truly, was not capable of grasping that actually there was just one single entrance, and I kept thinking that someone, Marina perhaps, was definitely upstairs; having used one of the five entrances, and now she didn't know that I was hunkered down in the lift wiping the snot from my nose on both sleeves. It had already grown dark; I was hesitating about where I should spend the night: the lift or the stairs, just to the left of the entrance. Finally they did come, but it was only after two days. I slept in the lift both nights. And when I ran into Marina's arms, dirty and snotty, into an embrace in fact, because of that slight, thin electrical current running out of her palms, she pinched my cheek roughly, in the roughest way you could imagine, like a bandit, actually, and she said: 'Don't make such a fuss! You weren't even waiting for an hour.' Then I started snivelling even more than before, all over the existing smeared and pasty snot on my face: 'I spent the whole day there and the whole night and then the whole day again and a whole night I slept alone in the lift and nobody, nobody came.'

Marina looked at Jaglika (encoded family glances) and said softly: 'This child's never going to stop lying. We're taking her to the doctor.'

V

The year is 1960-something; summer vacation in the Adriatic town of Poreč: Marina and her new husband (a very tall and insufferably suntanned guy, no great intellect, but, thank God, of very gentle disposition; when these two little things come together, when one giant meets another, although they are terribly at odds, the result obtained with gastronomical, that is, divine, skill, is dullness, a minor dullness or optimism, things that are six of one and half a dozen of another, in an unpleasant dosage) along with Danilo and I, of course; what a group! According to Marina's amazing plan, after our stay in Poreč we were supposed to make a four-part (there were four of us) hop over to Ljubljana, where Jaglika had moved after the arrival of the new husband; to live with God knows which relatives. The most straightforward exchange on God's green earth: Jaglika there, and the new fellow here. On the fifth day of the vacation, however, an incident took place that dispersed us in three different directions. The fault for our first (in our new composition) multilateral quarrel (all against all) lay in equal measure with two things: Marina's fantastic ass and the book *Netochka Nezvanova* – bound in navy blue linen with the title in gold letters; plus a man's hand, the one and the other like intervening factors in a large number of visible, invisible, and half-visible important and trifling phenomena. Actually, Marina and her new husband had a predilection for readerly perversions: one of them would read books aloud to the other, in the most varied situations, in varied bodily positions, weather conditions, or various states of mental anguish (it was way better than any of those ridiculous pills or psycho-relaxants). Accordingly, it was in one such circumstance (positioning of the body, weather, time) – the preparation of lunch in the kitchenette of the rented house in Poreč, with Marina's husband reading the aforementioned Dostoyevsky, when he let his other hand slowly work its way across Marina's fantastic ass. Her husband with *Netochka*, bound in blue covers, in his hand, and his other hand in exactly the right spot, as far as literature and the book were concerned, and life, too, Both hands in the right locations; the large oval protruding surfaces beneath the thin fabric of her bathing suit, coupled with Dostoyevsky; Marina, however, was gainfully preoccupied, focused on stirring with a wooden spoon, and holding dishes, which meant that the stove was on – besides the heat of the summer, electric heat – and, to be sure, listening to what her husband was reading, loudly and distinctly: 'Yes – said B. thoughtfully.' But no: he will wake up immediately. His madness is stronger than truth, and he will think up some excuse or other, right away. I was already in the kitchen, to which I had come not because of the reading or my mother's rear end: which was truly the whole event, but because I was terribly hungry, having just woken up a few minutes earlier. 'Do you think so? – remarked the prince.' (I was being completely quiet, enraptured with this scene; I hesitated in confusion for only a moment, and with both hands on my mouth: Oh, God, they've got a little burlesque thing going on here, how witty of them). The husband, appearing to skip over part of the book (Dostoyevsky, such a bore), continued reading in a raised voice: 'At last, Karl Fedorovich came running up, out of breath. He was carrying a sign. I tried very hard to hear everything…' Danilo came in (straight from swimming) and interrupted the magic. At first he was fuming with rage, and in the next moment he said very loudly (it was not screaming quite yet): 'Whore.' Marina's husband shut the book (secret sign) as if to catch a tossed ball (first gesture-reaction) and calmly placed it on the table and just as calmly (if not even more so) exited the kitchen (second reaction-protest). Then Marina (she was always last at everything) started towards Danilo (you could tell by her face, her extended fists, and her gait) with pugilistic intentions. Meanwhile I threw something out there – I've forgotten what, but at any rate it was something minor, a word of no consequence, but judging from everything it must've been in a nasty voice, for Marina, who had not noticed me at all up to that instant (it only seemed that way) turned around and hissed: 'It's always *you*…You're at the root of *allllll* of it!' Danilo, I presume, thought that all of Marina's pugilistic fury was going to shift to me, so he boldly, incautiously (doubtlessly) said through clenched teeth: 'You whore.' Then Marina's blow landed, from the side – on his neck, his ear, his temple. Everything was wrong: this whole trick: Marina had a right to her life, to her husband's hands, to *Netochka*, and, to be sure, to her own ass. But in the very next moment the two of them were going at it for real, yanking each other's hair and shoving each other towards the stove (what fiery desires!): I wasn't needed; but I, apparently, was affected: I dashed out of the kitchen to look for Marina's husband; I found him down at the beach (getting a tan) and for the next half an hour I tried without any success to convince him that he needed to make use of his influence over Marina.

The next day, Danilo took off for who-knows-where. I went back home. But Marina and her husband still went over to Ljubljana to see Jaglika and those relatives. That was just the beginning. The remaining year that the four of us lived together in Svetosavska Street saw daily fights. Typically, Danilo would say something about Marina's husband – something so insulting that the latter, following long-established habit – would disappear that same instant (second or third bedroom, the balcony, or the street), and then Marina and Danilo would exchange a few words before finally actually having it out. I behaved the same way Marina's husband did, with one difference: I didn't leave right off the bat, but I also didn't get involved. Later, Marina claimed that everything was my fault. That summer, while on their visit at Jaglika's, Marina managed to get several things done: everyone believed that my influence over Danilo was both obvious and sick, they knew very well where that came from, that is, from which side of the family and from which people within our family; furthermore, they all believed that my malice bordered on madness and that this was all connected with Marina's bottomless unhappiness. When they departed for Milan a year later, Marina and her husband, Jaglika came back from Ljubljana as fast as she could. It was on account of Danilo, as she said later: 'Don't imagine that things were bad for me there. They took care of me like I was the apple of their eye... Everything revolved around me... with every one of them offering favours... But I came back because of Danilo... You're a *bullshit-nik* just like he is... That much I know for sure.'

The 'he' here was my father; Jaglika would always talk like that. It was simpler: he, him. And by the way, those relatives in Ljubljana could hardly wait to have Jaglika off their backs.

For the first few months, Danilo spent a lot of time in Milan. I was also rarely at home; and Jaglika picked up a brand-new pursuit: she played cards day and night with this strange old man on the ground floor. Later on, the old guy died, and Jaglika was angry that I didn't go to the funeral with her. She got to know his relatives (who turned up on account of that ground-floor apartment), lost her marbles and kept inviting them repeatedly for coffee, and for this, and for that. These folks (husband, wife, and niece) regularly accepted Jaglika's invitations – in fact they didn't ever leave the house, I ran into them all over the place and at every time of the day – in the morning, in the evening, in the middle of the day, in the bathroom, living room, dining room, kitchen, in front of the front door, next to the door…

One night when I kicked them out, and things got all theatrical: shouting, oaths, curses, raised arms, it turned out that they knew everything about me: both the seen, and the unseen, the fictitious and the real; and more of the fictitious: the whole building hummed with various little stories. In fact Jaglika slandered me to the old man's relatives. This pure phantasmagoria: my hundred-year-old grandma, and those folks with their primitive physiognomy and needs to match, and me, their only connection, their reason for existing. Naturally, just this didn't frighten off Jaglika. She simply moved to the ground floor; and my threats to send her to Milan to be with Marina, or to Ljubljana to 'those super-duper relatives of yours', came to naught. She didn't stop chewing the cud with those ground floor dopes, for months, and even the building next door lived and breathed various little stories about morality and immorality. Then one day, these folks (the husband, wife, and niece), simply vanished, and I assume it was because they lost some court battle about the apartment. Jaglika came back depressed, and quarrelsome, and jumped all over me whenever I uttered a word; once again nothing was good enough, I was a bullshit-nik, a gypsy, a bum, and a 'super-whore' and 'that girl' and so on and so forth…

In the year 1970-something, everything was the same, or similar, which is the same thing when you're watching from the side-lines. My isolation was supplemented by letters from an anonymous author, about whom nothing was known: sex, age, inclinations, desires, origin, occupation, and the rest, but especially the rest – as is the case with all unknown authors, despite which everything appears to be authentic, so the only thing that's questionable is the fabrications of all kinds of (anonymous authors in all epochs; in all lands) in essence trivial people, although it is customary to think of these people (anonymous authors) as paranoid – which means danger, and to think of shutting them away, for example, in a prison or in a hospital or in both. Vespasian's letters appeared like a bolt from the blue; I don't know any other way to explain it; it's not necessary to explain it any other way; after all, Vespasian was himself a heavenly figure, and as for what objects become intermediary (postal-postmanly) there's no use racking one's brains about that! Doubts and, generally speaking, various outbursts of rationality and scepticism in regard to divinity, the heavens, heavenly figures, and letters, are not advisable, even if a letter is unnecessary; even if Vespasian is a pure fabrication. In any case, my reading of his letters, (which always arrived bearing no signature, with crumbs, fingerprints, and stains on them), can't be anything but superfluous to the same degree. No more or less so, exactly the same amount: identically so.

The Roman Vespasian was probably given his name by his mother; my Vespasian got his name according to some sloppy principle of association, occurring at the same instant, that is to say, when the letter arrived. It was so imbecilic and without imagination, like when someone unexpectedly gives you a Maltese terrier. What's the point here, and where are we going with this obvious insufficiency of imagination? One night (around the same time that this first imperial letter came in, if it wasn't that exact same night) I slept with a guy I'd picked up when I was wasted, in a café or on the street, I can't remember anymore. For the most part guys like that weren't so awful; however, when you take into account criteria of a more serious nature (which assumes that I rule out all sentimentality aimed at myself), he was incomprehensibly bad; but despite that, and some other things (sweat, stink, and stupidity) he was *simpático*, with his little pale red member, his large, protruding lower teeth, and his eyes that bulged just a touch; he was charming, despite being a dimwit, and after all what would intelligence mean to him in life – a big dick or at least a thick one, maybe, but brains? And that's how this name came to be, not because I thought that night that I was sleeping (I imagined) with Vespasian of Rome, by means of mysterious powers, but simply like this: a cheerful bucktoothed pope (the newspapers were chock-a-block those days with news about the pope) and then all at once *boom – Vespasian*.

I had found a solution to my paranoia: at the bottom of every letter I placed the signature: Vespasian. Sometimes in Cyrillic, some-times in Latin script; I was thinking that in that way anyone (but then again, who?) who might be searching with the pedantry of the police through my drawers, folders, and boxes, might get confused and thrown off the scent for at least a moment; he would have to wonder, at first, whether this 'Vespasian', sometimes Cyrillic and sometimes Latin, in both printed and cursive letters, now in red ink, now in blue or black, whether this wasn't some code and a subcode of that same code, and, then, whether or not I myself had written these letters to myself, or whether I'd written them (me again) with the intention of sending them to someone, and so on and on ...

Roman Vespasian had received, at the start of his imperial career, pulled out of a drum, like on a game show, Africa; later he fell on hard times and dealt in mules, but I'm willing to bet that at that point he knew an empire awaited him; he could tell everyone to fuck off. My Vespasian is an invalid; in his restricted province of life he has issues with his daughter, his wife, and himself, which is incomparably harder: the arc is smaller and, logically, the prospects are too. That other Vespasian had firm, short limbs, while this one of mine mentioned in several letters that as a young man he was tall, slender, smart, and handsome. Neither one of them should be believed.

Vespasian's letter:

Dear Lidia,

How are you? What are you up to? What's new? How is she, how are they, how are all your various theys? Dear Lidia, you have to believe me when I say that I'm hideously bored. Boredom is going to drive me crazy. Everything bores me, save these letters, which look non-existent after I write them, and I do not know whether they reach you and I also do not know whether you read them or whether you toss them, if that's the right word, into the furnace, for example; by and large this non-existence or more precisely the absence of the possibility of verification leaves me with some fantastic illusions, in addition, Lidia, which is not without importance in my immobile life, and, Lidia, then, or even because of that, I can imagine something. Do you understand, Lidia, that I actually imagine it all? And let me tell you something, Lidia, that I'm sure you don't know: maggots are very good to use as bait for catching smaller fish, fishlets, especially; like for example: the red-eyed tetra and the common rudd. The procedure is as follows (if one's intention is to catch both the red-eyed tetra and the common rudd, if that intention is a firm one, and unambiguous, as I said, with regard to both kinds of fish): you need to put a little piece of liver in a place where there are flies (that means anywhere, in other words, everywhere); so that the flies can place deep into the meat their discharge, which anglers call larva; those flies, then they slice the liver in question (meat) in several locations. Then you bury the little piece in the ground; Lidia, in just a few days the worms hatch; with them, or with horse leeches, or with a very young frog you can head to the river. You shouldn't get too into this, that is to say that, pathologically into it, ambitiously, over there on the river one cannot catch the beautiful bream, or the even prettier and more supple hake, but what's wrong with a common rudd, or, let's say, that intriguing eel, which is delicious to boot! But let's drop it. Now it's time for the off-season. For me it's always the off-season. As far as my wife is concerned, I've always been amazed at how she manages to find so much strength and stay so spry. It's as if, in accordance with the old African custom, when she was a child, when she was a little girl, all over her back and above her elbows they carved symbols, and later, Lidia, they rubbed these symbols with charred meat – it was a real animal – that had solid muscles, exaggeratedly adroit and flat when looked at in profile – that distinction (for it is a distinction) belongs to the same marvel: by way of symbols and carbonized meat. I would not have been astonished if it one day seemed as though a Hottentot woman had strangled this child of ours. She concocts stories; Lidia, try, in addition to the other things that you do in life, try, just casually, to destroy the magic that is the warmth of the uterus and the vagina and above all of the clitoris that trembles from inside (pure metaphysics), and then go on and open your windows wide in the dead of winter. Put away your blankets, all the bedspreads, just let the biting cold into the room all around you, around your body; and you'll see that everything, inside you, will stay warm, and only a penis, if one's in the vicinity, will be frozen; blue, and timorous; my wife tried this anecdote out on me. I've never put it to the test. She, however, claims that the warmth of a clitoris or a vagina is staggering, and that there's no magic involved; she says it's simply the definite, straight truth: the temperature of the sun, and then she says that I as a man have to sense this even without the windows being opened. For ages I've been unable to recall this temperature about which my wife speaks; I ejaculate transparent fluid in the bathtub, below the surface of the warm water, and in the shower, and I move on from there not unburdened in the least; once I got an engorgement of some kind, you know, and then no orgasm ever came. If my wife is to be believed, the clitoris has a transcendental power – it communes with God Himself… What other nonsense is she not telling me, Lidia, such as, for example, her true dilemma: is the penis of a fifty-year-old (she's thinking of me) a *deus ex machina* or a *deus absconditus*? At that point I told her that I had read, as you probably have also, Lidia, but she certainly has not (later this proved to be quite true), some essays with that same title, *deus absconditus*, in a newspaper – what this was about, I'm sure you remember, Lidia. And I said that I didn't remember whether it was connected to that; but my wife told me that some things come from inside and that she could guarantee one hundred per cent that the author of those essays was some fifty-year-old man; it turned out to be quite true: the writer actually was a fifty-year-old man; but if the title *deus absconditus* was referring to a penis, which is completely within the realm of possibility, I still cannot see what the dilemma is with the other part: *deus ex machina*, and, what's more, why is it only fifty-year-olds?

All of this is annoying, and boring, Lidia. I don't know what I'm supposed to get out of it. I know even less about what any of it has to do with me.

Goodbye, sweet little Lidia.

VI

Put not one, but two sizeable rocks in your pocket and hit the first dog you come across in both eyes; and then, when the beast is high-tailing it away, squealing, well, don't waste any time – get after him, d'you hear? A dog knows better than anybody where to flee to get out of shitholes on earth, in heaven, or in between.

This is the way I caught that more or less harmless STD: *Trichomonas vaginalis*. One night I got in late from a trip to Ljubljana, from visiting God-only-knows which relatives of mine; it had been something about some things for Danilo, and some documents, from Marina. There were no more buses in from the airport; but a taxi was sitting not too far away from the exit of the building; I got in and a tiff started immediately with this guy who was already in there, about which route the guy should take (the guy being the taxi driver), that is to say, whom he should take first, since we were going different directions; we cursed at each other all the way to the bridge; several times I demanded of the driver that he stop so 'this idiot' could get out and 'go on foot' and 'what kind of dirty trick is this' and once more 'so he can go to hell'. At a point only a hundred, or five hundred, meters from the bridge, however, he said: 'Drive to the Hotel Balkan.' At that same moment I said: 'Drive to the Hotel Prague.' It turned out to be the Balkan. What a shame about the Prague! My imagination was insufficient, and this whole combination was stupid: the airport, a fifty-year-old man, Hotel Balkan, and trichomoniasis. In contrast to Marina and her husband back then, way back then, in Poreč: *Netochka Nezvanova* and lunch and the two husbandly hands and Marina's big butt, and I didn't possess any imagination, not a bit, not as much as a child, not an ounce. That much is clear at least. Later I fell prey to the temptation (having been treated for trichomoniasis for months) to send to various people I knew a few vaginal secretions crumbled into an envelope, and smeared on paper – like on laboratory slides; with my signature under a microscopic bit of fungus: 'with love from Lidia'. Anyway, so the guy in the Hotel Balkan takes off his shoes right away, as if he were in the Prague, and barefooted but in his politician's suit he just plops into bed. Later it turned out that hiding beneath that politician's suit were orange underwear, a hairy back, a scar below one of the globes of his butt – long, moon-shaped – and a big purple cock plus the abilities, let's say… of a thirty-year-old. A month or so later, I saw him at the opening of an exhibition; he had some other folks I knew with him, and I waited till he was off by himself a little (ostensibly he was viewing the paintings) and then from behind his back and up close to his ear, right on his wrinkly, yellowish neck (this guy was shorter than me), I whispered: 'You pig.' He turned around, looked at me in surprise, and went on pretending to look at the pictures; he was wearing his politician's suit, the same one as in Hotel Balkan. If only I'd been able to spit on him, but in a way that no one could see, or been able to rub trichomoniasis like an abstract daub, for instance, all over his angular, attractive, old man's face, but in a way that no one would see. I wasn't able to do anything. May I be forgiven for my cowardice; he simply ran away, slipped out abruptly, and he wasn't to be found out in front of the gallery, nor on the second floor, nor out back in the restaurant, and not in the parking lot either; he disappeared. For the next couple of days I imagined that every grey head of hair on the street, and every striped politician's suit was him, and I'd shove my way through the crowd, really determined this time to fill his face with spit. I thought it would be obvious to everyone, on the outside (looking askance) that this whole confusion, and therefore this whole happening, had its origin in a few wrongly linked phenomena; the Hotel Balkan, and before it the airport, and after it the trichomoniasis. If it had been the Prague, everything would have been different, everything would have transpired differently, even if we'd taken a different route to get there.

Čeda of Little River came by after an absence of several years – that's how his non-appearance for a week, or maybe a day or two longer, seemed to Jaglika anyway. She asked him to tell her next time where he was going and for how long he wouldn't be available, so that she wouldn't worry, and so she wouldn't think he'd disappeared for good. Čeda grinned, shrugged his shoulders one more time, and repeated: 'No problem, granny! Don't you worry about anything!' On the fifth of March, Čeda was a whole hour late. By then Jaglika had already gone half-bonkers; when he got there, she demanded that we all go out to Košutnjak. Čeda arranged Jaglika in the front seat; Danilo and I sat in the back. Čeda the Flow was smoking, and somehow the ashes were always dropping onto the edge of Jaglika's coat; Jaglika frowned and with her left hand rhythmically (actually it was mechanically) knocked the ashes off her coat, all the way to our destination, even when Little River was no longer smoking and there weren't any more ashes. On the return trip, Danilo started in with his: 'So are you sure that we're not going to get into a crash?' Čeda, with a condescending smile: 'Sure? Nobody can be sure about anything, my boy. You can't ever really know anything.' After Danilo became flustered, Little River surprisingly enough suddenly appreciated something about Danilo's anxiety, and he began comforting him: 'Don't you worry a bit. I've been driving for ten years.' And then Danilo would say again: 'But you're not sure, isn't it true, that you're not sure, and nothing can ever be known?' A slightly annoyed Čeda pulled over to the side of the road, and now without any trace of condescension said: 'But I am sure, Danilo … Is he always like this?' All at once Danilo, with a big grin on his face, goes: 'Look, Lidia, what pastures, and you, you've been driving for ten years and you've never seen these pastures.' Of course it's a given – though not from outside – that there weren't any pastures there, but Čeda of Little River replied: 'For exactly ten years.' Danilo asked again: 'No more and no less, but precisely ten years?' And calmly, patiently, Čeda answered (he knew that Danilo would repeat this question several times before they got home): 'Exactly ten years, my boy, right down to the day and the hour.'

On the sixth of March I dreamt that Marina, Jaglika, one of Jaglika's relatives from Ljubljana who was ill-disposed to me, and I solemnly (we were carrying bouquets of flowers) went through the gates at the entrance to the New Cemetery: lots of people about; the entire graveyard forest was cut down, and along the paths, towards the French cemetery and the Russian monument, rubber boxes and short coloured plastic mats had been set up; there were several sealed wooden caskets somewhat farther on, to the left of the entrance; their lids were covered with light blue brocaded shrouds with tassels; Jaglika, Marina, and I approached a casket that was set aside, right next to a big wall, to the right of the entrance to the cemetery. Jaglika laid down flowers next to it, on the ground, and raised the lid; Marina, standing back a bit, said: 'How are you, Mihailo?' I squatted; in the coffin lay, judging from the name at least, my father. Jaglika and Mihailo, from out of the casket, were whispering to each other. Meanwhile Jaglika waved several times with her head and opened her arms; a bit later she said: 'Here, we've brought your little girl to you.' Before anything else, I noticed his huge wrinkled ear; his hair was gathered at the back of his head in a grey ponytail; his face I could not see at all; and then I caught sight of an arm moving beneath the quilt; yellow, wrinkled, then, and not as long as I'd thought it was at first, Mihailo's arm. Then we exchanged greetings; Jaglika, Marina, and some relative from somewhere kissed Mihailo on both cheeks; I stood precisely as far away from the coffin as his arms could stretch, I touched his fingers, and then I planted a kiss on his palm, and one more on his fingernails. I said courteously, the way Marina and Jaglika had taught me: 'Goodbye, and have a good day, sir.' A minute later, some flying dwarf from the time of Erasmus of Rotterdam lifted me into the air with the twisted tips of iron hooks dangling from the belt on his waist. Once again, a moment later, the dwarf set me down on the wall above a suitcase with my father in it. A lot of people were there: they were counting out loud and there were also some pretty little red cards on their upper arms. Jaglika and Marina made their way to somewhere outside the graveyard; I couldn't tell when they left.

When I woke up, I told Jaglika everything word for word, picture by picture, including the smallest scenes and even every seemingly insignificant detail. Jaglika heard me out attentively and said: 'Pray to God that it's because you don't believe, and he didn't believe either and that is precisely why he went through what he went through, and all of it was because you don't believe; neither he nor you can blame anybody else, and again, it doesn't bode you two any good; it's no good at all … ' That was when I saw my father for the first time; later, much later (that little word 'much' is necessary because of the utter vagueness of temporal distances: I need to use it more times than I can count, but since that is impractical for obvious reasons, then a certain number of times will suffice as an indication of something infinite) much later I had the same dream again with some varying details; that's when I saw my father a second time; the third time that I saw him was on the street, directly opposite the library, where some or other person was transformed into him for just a moment, right before my eyes. This was genuine, or at least I thought it was. When I told Jaglika about it, she said once more: 'That's bodes no good for you.'

On the 7ᵗʰ of March, at 10:00 in the morning, Marko rushed into our house. Marko was Danilo's friend from secondary school. He usually came on Friday afternoons; he had a key. It was all a dull, repetitive story, year after year: let's say it was winter: Marko would come running into the house, red-skinned and frozen, with his nose running; with a big plastic bag in his hand. He lived in a shack, in a courtyard on Birčaninova Street. He got a decent amount of money from his parents, who lived in another city; nonetheless he was forever doing something on the black: trading in pornographic films, banned books from every corner of the globe, typewriters, tape recorders – things he never managed to sell, and, over time, adding machines and all kinds of other crap, so that he never had anything left over for the heating: there in that shack he would wrap himself up in rolls of toilet paper – which he always carried off from our house. Danilo bought every book that Marko brought by, and every porno film; eventually he also bought a movie projector. One month when we were totally broke, and actually in the red, Marko contributed the money he'd made on a few sales.

At school, they simultaneously gave Marko a bunch of different names: Eyepiece, Rat, Criminal; the nickname 'the Bag' he got as a present from Danilo. It was March 7, and I had not gone to work. When Marko came running in, the first thing he did was wake me up: he sat on my bed, rustled around with his bags (this time there were two other ones, in addition to the obligatory one), spat this way and that through the gaps in his teeth, and whooped: 'Come on Lida, get up!' (With his filthy hand he grabbed the thick quilt, underneath which he could not even see me, nor I him, and shook it.) 'I brought you something. It's super, Lida! Come on, Lida, make me a coffee, and then I'll have to run ... I don't have much time ...'

The unavoidable, unerring Marko the Bag, always in a hurry and always arriving at an ungodly hour, is sitting on my bed; I'm asleep; I stay asleep; and he says, 'Lida, I have a thousand and one things to do today. I can't wait!' I extricate my head, and then my arms from the quilt and in that instant I wake all the way up because of his gushing, spit-covered stare (it looked like a huge amount of snot or saliva had been smeared across his face) – from beneath those thick lenses (Marko was blind, so to speak; he saw nothing in the heavens or below them, only tiny shadows) or because of the stink of his mouth, his body, or both of them together? Anyway I was awake enough right then for it to seem like I would never again fall asleep in my life, not if Marko the Bag were sitting on my bed. I dragged myself out, with the speed of a big-ass otter (although it was more Marko who resembled an otter, with his snout, and not me) and I sat there for a moment or two, definitely no longer, with my legs gaping wide, rubbing my eyes, right beside stinky Marko the Bag. Meanwhile he was muttering like a madman: 'Lida, hurry it up ... I have a thousand and one errands to run.' Then he asked: 'Is Danilo ... not up yet?' I answered kindly, with a smile even, because of the good breeding I inherited from Jaglika and Marina – two fine city ladies: 'No, he's not. Go wake him up, Marko!' I should have screamed: Get lost, you bug-eyed retard, take a hike, beat it, who told you to come over anyway, you shithead... but I didn't, because of my good upbringing. I repeated: 'Go wake him up!'

Then Marko the Bag Rat Eyepiece Criminal, spraying the whole room with his vile saliva responded: 'You wanna get dressed? Should I leave?' He ran his tongue over his thin upper lip: I lunged for the bathroom and as soon as I made it – started to puke big-time. An agitated Marko shuffled back and forth in the hallway, whining like a tortured puppy and saying over and over: 'Good Lord... Good Lord, Lida, what's wrong with you... Lida, what did you eat? It must be something you ate... Lida, are you OK?' I waved him away and croaked, faintly: 'Go wake up Danilo!' Then I was sick again.

After his coffee, Marko, who had until that moment been sitting on the edge of his chair, fidgeting, got to his feet and began impatiently pulling things out of the bag: four pairs of spectacles, two chunks of mouldy bread, an onion, an entire cucumber, a little ham wrapped in opaque paper, pieces of string, a couple of reels of film, notes from a maths class, three books about the study of psychology, and a duplicated text about archaeological finds in Macedonia. Marko was studying archaeology, psychology, and maths all at once, and, what was most remarkable: sport and physical education. With the exception of the films, he put all the items back in the bags. 'Marko, do you want some breakfast?' – I asked him. He wasn't hungry; and he hurriedly cued up one of the reels on the projector that Danilo had brought in the meantime from his room. 'So you can see a super porno, Danilo. I've never seen anything better!' But the film was boring, horribly boring, just like all the other ones that Marko had brought. I walked out of the kitchen, got my bike, and went outside. Marko called after me, crestfallen: 'But Lida, this is the best one I've ever come across. If you only knew how much I paid for it *Lidaaa*!'

VII

At the beginning of April, Little River came over with Milena; he twisted at the waist, pulled his head into his shoulders, smiled as condescendingly as ever, and said: 'This is my good friend Milena… And this is Lidia, and Danilo. I was telling you about them. Now come meet Granny …'

Until then, Čeda of Little River had shown up daily on Sveto-savska to sit; one day Jaglika had a cold, another time she had a headache, on a third day it was her stomach, but Čeda came all the time anyway; he drank coffee with Danilo; read newspapers that he was never the one to purchase; kept asking if we'd like to buy a Japanese upright piano for cheap, some goat suet, also on the cheap, car tyres even cheaper, a complete set of the photo magazine 'Football' totally gratis and a hundred other marvels. 'But, Lidia, you'll never have another opportunity like this – it's an awful piano, so it's important that you don't know how to play; you will never be able to buy one so cheaply!'

I think Danilo fell in love with Milena the moment he caught sight of her blonde hair, round face, and big chest. For me, though, it took a few days (exactly as many days as Milena turned up with Čeda, to drink coffee, talk, and do whatever the hell else the two of them and all of us got up to in the apartment on Svetosavska) to discover, to realize, that the corners of Milena's mouth rose considerably when she smiled (a child's hand draws a half-moon the same way, horizontally and with pointy ends) and that the same thing that was happening to Danilo was also happening to me.

From that moment (when Milena entered our Svetosavska home bashfully) onward (and then when it all looked immovable and enduring) Milena just walked in, she didn't ring the bell, she didn't knock, and right from the doorway she began talking; the first thing you saw, the first thing anyone in the world would see, were the raised outlines of Milena's lips, like a hiked-up skirt revealing a glimpse of leg, (hers, of course), the knit fabric of her socks, and a great flash: 'Lidka, do you know what happened to me… I was at the dentist's. I had to wait three hours before I did anything else… and when I finally got to my place in that chair, you know, I closed my eyes in fear. You get it – I always close my eyes, clench my fists, I totally, Lidka, totally tense up my entire body, it's like I clench my face into a metal rod or a fist, and then for sure it must just look lumpy and… and so contorted… Then it has to be Lidka the ugliest face in the world, but no, not in the world, but anywhere ever… and while I'm gawking in that dentist's chair, I'm sitting there all tensed up and waiting… and then first of all I feel a soft touch and that's them tying the white cloth around your neck and then they usually catch your hair in those nickel-plated clips, and then out of the dentist's mouth it comes… and my eyes are shut the whole time, squeezed shut, all I can do is hear, in truth, what comes out of his mouth: 'Nothing to be afraid of we'll go nice and easy here.' And then, Lida, usually at a moment like that I can also hear little metallic sounds, you know them, the little mirror, the pumps and the other blah-blah-blah and then, Lida… It's unbelievable but instead of all that I hear somebody like, you know, murmuring something near my face, somebody, you understand, whispering something totally unintelligible, moistly, and instead of the drill and pumps, a little later, in my mouth, the dentist's huge slimy tongue, Lidka, it was awesome ... for a moment my mouth was puffed up by the dentist's tongue and by those cellulose pads and I couldn't breathe for just a moment ... But it all lasted for only a second, no, no, but even so it had been a good several seconds when the dentist pulled out his tongue. I opened my eyes and with my fingers I fished out the pads and started to giggle, and Lidia if you only could have seen that perfectly confused, 100 per cent confused dentist's face in that instant, he was holding those you know little tools and in a whisper, he totally like whispered a couple of times that we should get together later that day, it was mandatory that we see each other ... and then I, Lidka, just imagine, it's like, it was hideous, I had to try so hard not to burst, I mean just straight up burst into laughter, and then I just told him sweetly, coquettishly, you know what I mean, you know how it's supposed to go, otherwise they get pissed off, and Lida he definitely would have been angry. I told him that first he should fix my left #6, my right #3 ... and then we'll see about a little rendezvous and then I added once more terribly flirtatiously, that I didn't have anything against that ... So, you know, Lida, in truth I have nothing against it, but on the contrary, it would only be like I'd love to postpone it till after the six and the three and the four and so on, in general ... And then, Lida, he got down to business: first of all he washed out of my mouth with that spluttering little pump all the slime and spit since a lot of his spit was in my mouth, I had never seen before, swear to God, seen, and I mean I have never seen, like, I didn't know that so much spit could be secreted, as if he were a dog, Lida it was so totally loco, I thought that I was going to drown for a second, just for a second ... and when he washed everything out of my mouth that way, and with the pads tremendously carefully wiped the remnants of the water off my chin, he picked up the drill and repaired one of my whole teeth, a half hour, I didn't get up for a half hour, it was unreal, and then Lida, when I started moving to leave, he stood like two meters away from me as if he'd become scared and it was crazy unpleasant for him, and Lidia I seriously thought, first the teeth and then the rendezvous, and he, do you understand Lida, he was beetroot-red and then, a moment or two later, while the nurse was scheduling my follow-up, you understand, when I said goodbye and the rest of it, you know already, he said not a word, nothing at all and so, Lida, it was great fun, the most fun imaginable, if you don't count the overabundance of spit, but I don't understand why he changed his mind once things were rolling… Lida …'

When she finished telling me the story about the dentist's tongue and all the rest of it, Milena was already naked, with skin that glowed in all directions and filled the entire room, and it took my breath away for a moment, just like with all fools in similar situations, or better: like all fools who have anything to do with Milena, with Milena's skin; and besides that there was the chill of the room; Milena had goose bumps, and so it looked like the tiny needles on her skin very nearly blocked off the entire room. A few moments later, after I lost my head just as the dentist had done, Milena said brusquely, in a commanding tone, that she wanted to sleep and that I should stop delaying, a big job was waiting, but what job (asks the prisoner – me), and my master (Milena) lifted yet again (the corners of her mouth as if this were about her skirt, exactly like that), stretched out beneath my awkward and unnecessary arms, and went to sleep; very quickly I felt the pins and needles start in my arm, but I was unable, yes, I simply could not be so bold as to pull it out, take it away, to save it from this great white load – the whole of untouched Milena, because she would wake up just as easily as she fell asleep. And the anger of the master and the humility of the slave, of course, work just like that; so then it's better like this: a numbed arm, underneath the master's back.

VIII

DANILO'S FLY

Soaked, wet through and through, I go into the house; it's Friday; no! It's Thursday; fine, I don't actually know what day it is; what anything it is; year, season, whichever one it is; location – more of the same – Svetosavska – library, and Svetosavska Street again, and then that little space in between, which I cross every blessed day with my head bowed, my glasses on the end of my nose, and deafened by the steps, the very steps, steps of hurrying humans; my head is bent so that these human figures won't see me, my glasses too, not for that reason but more for reasons of common courtesy: my head up and no glasses on my nose and, of course, footfalls that were a little bit softer – and everyone would drop dead, they'd all keel over on the pavement from hatred of my face; me, I know that this persistence, with hardly any patience (that signifies foolhardiness) will indeed one fine day end up being rewarded by God: they'll writhe around, each in their turn, on the pavements, in that same small space, between Svetosavska and my library; nevertheless. It's the same (and that's exactly why): library, Svetosavska, day, night, noon, a brief twilight, autumn, an excursion with Čeda, Jaglika, Danilo, and now with Milena – what an ostensibly family gathering: artificial flowers in little glass bottles.

And so, I arrived, and that means from work – that's the only clue as to the time of day: four or five in the afternoon – the precise time cannot be determined with any certainty; Danilo got up a little before that; Jaglika was still sleeping – on Svetosavska Street, everyone slept through the day and night, and both of them, the two of them (everyone) never failed to recount how they had not slept a wink all night, all day, and then for another whole night, and my God, in truth there is no worse fate than insomnia. At home naturally, there was nothing to eat; and Danilo, astonished, like always, to see me at all, and amazed as he was at so many other things, at all other things, rubbing his eyes with the insides of his fists, and asking at the same time: 'But why are you wet, Lidia… my *Goood* but you are wet it's pouring off you Lidia and *Lidiaaa*… why are you standing there… you'll ruin Marina's parquet floor… my *Goood* Lidia how'd you get that drenched?' Rivulets of water were flowing off me; tremendous puddles of water were spreading across Marina's all-important floor, which only Danilo spent serious time reflecting on, of course, and there was no reason for me to ask whether there was any lunch to be had; naturally, Lord knows and it goes without saying, there was no lunch; for days and days on end Jaglika ate nothing but apples, and quinces, and more apples and a litre of yogurt, Danilo didn't eat anything at all; what would that puny creature, maybe just over five feet tall, do with even a crumb of food; when as a child he was pressed to eat everything on his plate, Danilo would with great difficulty swallow what he had already stuck in his mouth, as if it were nothing but shit – and he made such a face and in secret he would spit out the two remaining morsels (in his mouth) in the direction of the window and say, over and over again, he'd mumble: 'and if I want to stay a runt, what's wrong with that, it's actually better… ' He actually turned out a bit better, 160 centimetres, 5 feet 2 inches, and of course it wasn't on account of the food left on his plate, nor because of the morsels he discharged from his mouth through the window – in the direction of the washed and unwashed heads of the passers-by – in the morning – like morning Communion: what's wrong with it, nothing's wrong with it, it's actually better; and what does food mean to him now, if in fact it was out of fear that he left food behind on his plate, all of Jaglika's famous dishes, with caraway seeds – for one's stomach, and with a bit of horseradish in them – against colds. And then, then there was something else here, with regard to this height of five-odd feet. I will truly never get why Danilo, for years, when he was little, would get up in the middle of the night, put his coat on over his pyjamas, and his shoes on his bare feet, and angry, every night try to go outside. He was actually angry about something; I know this wasn't a matter of walking in his sleep; Danilo had insomnia – more precisely, up until the moment he went outside, he was awake. After the beating he'd get, regularly, for doing that, every night, I mean for years, Danilo would say something more or less like this: 'Throw me into the well, if I'm so useless, if I'm just the worst thing ever. At least it will feel tight there and narrow, narrow, and I won't have to look at your shitty faces. You make me vomit.' After that he'd get another and more serious beating, and after neither the first, nor the second set of blows elicited even the tiniest tear in at least one of his eyes (stupid old Marina interpreted crying as repentance and humiliation, and she liked it), Marina would wrap up the entire incident (things almost always took this same turn, year after year) with a single sentence, with something at last sensible: 'Fine. We're going to throw you in the well.'

'You could have bought something to eat!' I say to Danilo, and don't budge from Marina's parquet floor.

'What the hell, like, can't you see that I just woke up a little bit ago? And why are you so hideously wet? I've never ever seen such a thing, geez, Lidiaaa!?'

'It's raining, you idiot.'

'Really? Why didn't I think of that!'

'My boss hosed me down with his whole load of backed-up sperm, through his eyes, you know, he ejaculated right through his *eyesss*.'

'Oooh! That means he's cured of his Graves' disease!'

'He never had it, you dimwit.'

'Lidia, you've told me that at least ten times. Lidia, stop making me crazy, for Pete's sake. You've told me a million times or more how he's got a baggy ass and short legs and blah blah blah you told me all sorts of other nonsense about that miserable guy… I can imagine what he thinks of you… not even a dog would—'

'Shut it. I told you that he looks that way, do you understand, you cretin, that he looks like that. It just looks like that. I never said to you that he has it and anyway I couldn't give a rat's ass about Graves' disease or about you or anything, d'you hear… !'

All the water had obligingly drained off me; now I was dry; Marina's poor parquet floor; poor Danilo; poor Jaglika, she's going to slip and break her arm, or her leg; she'll break both her arm and her leg, which is best of all, which would make you simply keel over with happiness; I ran down the stairs, the very thought of a broken Jaglika filled me with unbelievable vigour, taking the steps at a leap two by two, and suddenly three at a time, and at the bottom even four; when I returned with paper bags and food, Danilo was still standing there, next to those puddles, confused and, for all I know, determined to have the last word about my boss's eyes, to wit:

'Lidia, it amounts to the same thing. You know it's the same; I was thinking about it, and it's completely, like, totally, the same thing, you see, Lidia? Whether your boss has Graves' disease or if it just seems like he does.'

'Wanna eat, Danilo? Go ask Jaglika, if she's awake …'

'Lidia, come on and say it. It's totally the same thing, eh, Lidia?'

'All right; they're the same. Get this water cleaned up, Danilo. For goodness' sake. Get cracking.'

'Well, first I have to go to the bathroom.'

'Listen, Danilo, what did you do all day, Danilo, what do you do for such long stretches of time … ?'

After a full half hour (precisely half an hour) Danilo came out of the bathroom; I'm a hundred per cent sure he was wanking off, because he let the water run the entire time.

'Danilo, go see what *Baba's* up to … she's not making any noise … maybe she's dead. Danilo, go see what Jaglika is doing and again – wipe up that water, okay, Danilo!'

Another full half hour – no! It simply drives a person crazy! – and he's flopping around, and he simply drags himself through the house loaded up with brightly coloured rags that look like remnants of Marina's dresses and with a grin (this is in fact a bit of 'mama's little man, mama's little sweetie') on his face, and eyes clear and rinsed: 'Lidia, I know you're sorry to hear it, but *Baba* isn't dead. Just so you know, she's sleeping like a new-born baby.'

'What did you do all day?'

'You're going to make fun of me if I tell you.'

'I won't. C'mon, Danilo. Tell me!'

'But you'll ridicule me, I know you. I know you, Lidia.'

'You have my word. I won't. Now come on …'

'Oh, okay. But you're sure you won't make fun of me?'

'Really, I won't.'

'When you left for work, I gave Jaglika her yogurt, etc., and then I sat right down to have me a nice little breakfast but Jaglika kept calling out, my glasses, my this, my that, imagine, Lidia. She was sitting on her glasses and they didn't break.'

'Well, they're plastic.'

'And as I told you, I was just sitting there, making a cup of tea and so forth, when a fly flies up. I chased it for two whole hours, but no… several hours… One moment it was here, right here, Lidia, and then there, and after that in the living room, and then in the foyer, and Lidia, once more imagine – it was several hours – once more it was right here, do you understand, just like this on the edge here, and my tea had gone all cold and so on, and later it was like it'd vanished, and so on, I take a bit of my bread and butter, and it came back and stopped right there… do you see, right there, Lidia…'

'You're saying it landed? Where?'

'Well, there, on the dishrag, and I was puking, d'you know, I couldn't swallow a bite of anything else anymore, I flat-out had to throw up, the whole day, and just now, before you got there, I was vomiting constantly, every ten minutes, it was flat-out horrible, Lidia, it was like I was going to die, I didn't eat anything, Lidia, but I swallowed that fly… Lidia… but Jaglika said to me this morning that no harm will come to me, and she also said I should imagine that it's healthy, that it was healthy for me, Lidia…'

'Well, okay, Danilo, did you vomit it up?'

'How should I know? I didn't check, Lidia, I couldn't look at all that green and yellow, it would make me nauseous again, I haven't stopped vomiting, the whole time, since this morning, Lidiaaa…'

'Jesus, Danilo, why didn't you check for it? Why didn't you look?'

'Lidia, it's a terribly small fly, not the regular kind at all, and why are you shouting again, why? I vomited the whole day and you are screaming. What were you gaping at… What's the matter with you… even now I'm feeling its little tiny legs here in my throat it can't work itself free but everything went over it, that stuff from last night, the slop you cooked up last night… it had gone bad… not even a dog would've… and I didn't see it, you know, it was already too late when I noticed I saw it only belatedly… what are you gawking at… why are you playing dumb here… like this could never happen to you… It's when you see it but in fact you don't know you've seen it and in fact you don't remember, know what I mean, Lidia, afterwards I remembered, after I had seen it, and Jaglika was giggling… what is it, what are you staring at… ?'

'Danilo, how do you know you swallowed it?'

'I swallowed it with my tea, how, how do I know? I know full well; I didn't see it anywhere, I didn't see it here in the house anywhere again, what's wrong, why are you staring at me, what is it, Lidia?'

'You fabricated all this. You didn't swallow the fly, you idiot.'

'I should think I'd know… I guess I know whether I swallowed it or not… I'd probably feel it… I do feel it, here… You drive me bonkers, Lidia… Not even a dog would… This is terrible. I'm going to write to Marina… Lidia, you drive me crazy…'

'Oh, get over it. That's enough hysteria for now. Go get Jaglika up. It's eight o'clock already.'

IX

The next day, Danilo and I went to see Mira, Danilo's girlfriend; we didn't catch her at home; Danilo said she'd 'left to go have it out with that cretin'. On our return journey, Danilo slapped the woman conductor; and then, when the people all around them started shrieking, screaming, baying: 'Call the police… Call the police… Get that lunatic out of here… People like that should get hanged out on Terazije… ' and when even I could no longer protect him from the conductor who almost bit his head off, Danilo started crying. Maternally, the conductor opened the doors; we got out, followed by curses, blows, spit, and the rest of it. We walked the remainder of the way home on foot. Danilo never ceased crying, and he never, ever ceased repeating, quietly and monotonously, the same thing – through his tears: 'It's not like I robbed somebody or anything like that.'

We witnessed this scene in Svetosavska: Milena, Milena in the flesh and, nothing but Milena whispering with Jaglika; actually, it was just Milena whispering and Jaglika nodding her head, as if someone had installed a battery in the vertebrae of her neck, in fact, like a mechanical Schweik, the good soldier, in a wheelchair. When Danilo sprang up to give her a kiss, she snapped rudely at him: 'Danilo, you stink like a public toilet. Go brush your teeth first, and then come see me!'

She pushed Jaglika, Jaglika and the wheelchair, into another part of the flat. She closed behind herself and behind Jaglika two, not three doors (and Jaglika blows her top and keeps moving her head like Schweik), and began to whisper incoherently: 'Lidka listen Lidka sex in little steady doses that's one thing, regular intervals, but you know this already … antibiotics … and such not … marriage … and you know … you've been married … it's just that … injections of sex straight into your brain … everything in its time that's one thing a little lunch a little sleep a little screwing everything in its time God forbid not at awkward times, and a little work and then some of that other, on Sundays a bit earlier, you know, it's like … the next day you have to work… and you screw around at seven in the evening or even better a touch of wine after lunch and then you do it right after lunch so you don't lose a day of rest… Isn't that right Lidka you have to do it this way too … That other thing, Lida… you don't have the imagination for it in fact, for you it's just like you're masturbating, it's like your other hand is a little dick you simply don't see it and it got smaller in marriage, didn't it, but Lidka, tell me, isn't it so, it was regular but you were still alone, and Lida, and wasn't it like that for you, I'll bet that you were, and that other stuff was boring, deadly boring, so boring that you cracked from boredom, all the orgasms were boring, always the same thing, but Lidia, there are always more orgasms than you can shake a stick at, but it makes you sick, your stomach always turns, Lida, come on and say it, Lida, that's how it is, well, Lida, for God's sake, admit it!'

'Shut up, Milena; shut your trap!' – I slammed the fourth door; after that you could hear a fifth – Milena had left; but just a few moments later, Milena returned. She'd forgotten to kiss Danilo (Danilo was being a complete and non-stop cry-baby). In the meantime he'd brushed his teeth thoroughly; I assume that over there in the corner Milena is still whispering, and that Jaglika, over there somewhere in her wheelchair, is continuing to nod her head, like Schweik, and both of them thinking the same damn thing in their illiterate brains about how orgasm is, obligatorily, a matter of imagination and not habit. Milena was in love; of course, I didn't sense that at first; I needed a lot of time, like I always do, with everything; I underestimated Milena, I thought that her cluelessness on all fronts was incomprehensibly small; I thought that above all she was untrained in the conditioning of her own experiences, through another person (the other person was necessarily suffering), I had an informal notion of her: and by that I mean she was: indifferent, of unvarying comportment, a touch melancholic, completely balanced, and I liked that kind of Milena, no less than I like a good lunch or some sound, iron-clad sleep!

X

Marina, my mother, had two brothers; in addition to having hate-filled dreams about them, I also had real experiences with them when I was a child. In fact, those experiences form part of my 'liberated' memory.

At the time, the two of them lived here; they used to come periodically to our place on Svetosavska Street, and their thousand and one pieces of junk would come with them – oh, screw it – they never brought anything; they came over and gossiped and ran off at the mouth, spitting, chomping, and, like everybody in the building on Svetosavska, shamelessly exploiting pathetic, beleaguered old Jaglika: she cooked for them, washed, cleaned, and, to top it all off, we took her pension for ourselves; she took care of all of us on Svetosavska Street, languished, day and night, and declined, inevitably declined. We bustled here and there and didn't even take her on an outing, not to mention a summer vacation.

First I dreamt about my maternal uncle, F. He was the older one, taller and skinnier than Uncle K. It was approximately a year ago, and the long and short of it was this: in his room – in his house in Ljubljana (both of them live there now) – I killed him, with a listless movement of hand and knife; there wasn't terribly much blood; he was standing with his back turned to me and the patio and an important picture on the wall – everything simultaneously: picture, patio, me, and my uncle's back; I couldn't resist,

and why would I? I stuck him with the short blade, planted it right
in the centre, between those shoulder blades of his that I thought
were too close together (that's how skinny he was), noiselessly and
effortlessly: Uncle K didn't make a sound; then, somehow – I've
always known that I was as strong as a horse, and that there are
things that I could handle that not even a horse could, and not
even in a dream could a horse carry such things… I carried him
onto the terrace, where a great cauldron was already set up over a
fire (like in a fairy tale); I thrust him in and cooked him, until the
water (his blood) turned completely white – now that was some
wondrous alchemy! Afterwards his body grew stiff and shrank –
the handle of the knife, however, was still jutting out, completely
undisturbed, from the middle of his narrow, gaunt back, like from
the centre of the cosmos. I removed him from the cauldron – he
had been reduced in size so much that I only needed to use one
hand – as if I were picking up a big loaf of black bread, let's say – in
the grocery store; I've known for ages that I'm actually as strong
as, oh, a mouse – and I slung him up onto the railing and shoved;
a hundred years after that, some people appear, let's say they rep-
resent the 'dream police' – they're all sweet, sympathetic, but also
pretty shrewd, something that was very much in evidence after
these one hundred new years: they asked if I had any ties to the
doll made of rubber that was down there in the garden; by that
I mean down there in the park; what connection did I have to
this figure made of some odd composite that was so irresistibly
reminiscent of Mr F? I betrayed my own secret to them, naturally
enough: I said that the doll down there, of rubber, was the head
of my former uncle F, of flesh and blood. Several of them smiled,
and then off they went, all together. After three hundred more
years, they returned; and now Marina was with them. She was

the first, and this can be attributed to her innate pedantry, to see the great stain on the carpet in the bedroom – the room in which Uncle F had had a knife stabbed into the middle of his back. It was, I assume, my uncle's blood – which must have been dripping, leaking out of the wound the whole time, until I transferred him, with the strength of a horse and a mouse simultaneously, from the room to the terrace – and into the cauldron.

My dream about the other uncle took place in circumstances that were no less grim. All the relatives had gathered for a family celebration – there were so, so many of them that they seemed to spill out like ants into Svetosavska Street – both the living and the dead. Uncle K, who was younger and heavier than Uncle F, I castrated with a razor blade; although I'm no longer sure whether it was a razor blade or a pair of those scissors for clipping nails; but it seems most likely that there was a dark brown penknife in my hands – in one hand, just in one hand. First we all played some dreary party game: we hid ourselves in all possible locations. A few of them hid in the wardrobe; Daniel's and my clothes started falling out; in that part of the dream, a towering burst of rage came over me: I attacked people, with the intention of throwing them out of the wardrobe, or out of the house; After Marina intervened, they remained, there at Svetosavska Street, but now they were hidden; instead of being in the wardrobes and cabinets, they were under all the tables; as if it were a present, I got a dangerous look from Marina – which had to mean, and still does mean, this – 'if you dare do it, I'll kill you after they leave, you little bastard, you scourge of God!' The next dream sequence, the main one, actually, was: sexual intercourse with Uncle K, and immediately afterwards the castration; he didn't make a peep, just as Uncle F didn't, when I stabbed that knife into the middle of his back. Uncle K's phallus was wrapped up in a wad of rags; nicely, that is to say politely, and that means in a soft (courteous) voice, I asked Jaglika to toss it down the garbage chute when she went out. Jaglika merely nodded her head and crammed her son's phallus into her pocket. After that point, the events got less dramatic: Marina's husband showed up in a clean white shirt and a tie with dots all over it (red and blue, quite the prosaic combination) and a pipe in his mouth, to boot. In the corner of the room an unknown woman was seated; she was wearing an old-fashioned evening gown and sitting right below the portrait of a man on the wall who was also unfamiliar to me. When I caught sight of them, I went directly over (both to the man in the photo on the wall, and the woman underneath the photo); and a moment later I took down the picture, sliced it into pieces (but I carefully set aside the pane of glass) and then began making a few pictures of my own – which I then later glued to the table. Jaglika in a tuxedo, although perhaps it was Marina, I don't know. Marina was more corpulent, wider, as if she'd been inflated. She was pulling me out onto the dance floor, and ultimately I felt like we were just hopping around in front of the woman in the ball gown.

Once, a long while after that, when I told Danilo's doctor about this dream, he said to me – and good Lord I never doubted his skill, even if I did harbour suspicions about his potency; most assuredly I had no doubts about his skill – he told me that the picture on the wall and in my head was actually my father, and that cutting it up was the expression (what an expression!) of my ambivalence towards my father; and then he went on to tell me that the woman in the evening gown beneath the picture was in part my mother, and in part not, and it was even to a small degree me. Psychiatrists, not all of them, but for sure all the stupid ones, and thus all of them, come to think of it, simply pull a formula out of thin air, as casually as if they were striking a match or having a bowel movement: ambivalence and so forth, right on down the line.

But what was it that happened involving me and Marina's two brothers, the skinny, older one F, and the chubby younger one, K? One day, F and K burst (with the best of intentions in their hearts) into the place on Svetosavska: from the moment they crossed the threshold, they were strutting around and bragging about their plans for that afternoon; it was a Sunday, and I think it was at the beginning of spring. They had come to pick up Jaglika, Danilo, and me to take us to Topčider Park. We took a taxi; or, I mean, actually, we should have gone by taxi. From Svetosavska Street all the way to the National Theatre we went on foot, sometimes on the pavement and sometimes in the middle of the road. Danilo was ten at the time, and I was eleven. The first thing we did was go into a cake shop, there in the vicinity of the theatre. I was looking for some cream pie, and Danilo wanted angular baklava and oblong *tulumba*. Uncle F (he's the older and leaner one, with the knife in the middle of his back) said, while Jaglika stood there drinking some *boza*: 'That's a lot, Danilo … You're going to get a stomach ache.' Then Danilo demanded two more *šam-rolna*, foam rollers. I ate two pieces of *šampita*, whipped cream pie, as I mentioned (earlier, at the beginning), and then I was just sitting in a corner of the nearly empty sweetshop, rocking back and forth in a chair. Now Jaglika got herself a lemonade, too (what the heck!); Uncle K was sucking in the smoke from one of his *Drinas*, a brand of cigarette from Sarajevo, while sitting directly below a sign stating that smoking was prohibited. Then F, the older one, said yet again: 'That's too much, Danilo. You're going to get a stomach ache. You'll see!' But once more Danilo asked for some cake; he wouldn't stop chewing and smacking his lips, so that I had to think that after this Sunday morning there wouldn't be a single serving of cream puffs left, or baklava, either Greek or Turkish, or *krempita*, for the children who'd be coming by later. Now the pastry chef placed two pieces of chocolate cake and two mignons of fruit and candy on a plate in front of Danilo; and Danilo spotted the hair, long, black, and sturdy (as if it were from Uncle K's head, which was, truth be told, impossible, completely ruled out by the fact that Uncle K was standing a good two meters away from the plate, and from Danilo, and from the pastry chef; however you chose to look at it, that is to say, however one might measure that distance – it was not possible that a hair from the head of Uncle K could have found its way to Danilo's plate and assumed this position across those two mignons). The only link that could be established between the hair in question and Uncle K was the marvellous similarity of the hairs on his head and the one on Danilo's plate. It certainly did not belong to the baker; his hairs were light brown, thin, and soft. I believe that Danilo would've passed over it in silence if the hair had come from the pastry chef's head; but because it could not have been thus, he was convinced that Uncle K had deliberately placed the hair on his plate, and he couldn't restrain himself, I know it; he could not do so by any means, and what happened later was necessary; things just had to happen like that. And so, when Danilo caught a glimpse of the long, black, thick hair on the plate (I also saw it at the same moment, and I assume that no one aside from the two of us saw it), he cupped his hand, very calmly, over the mignons and the pieces of chocolate cake, and he simply wiped them silently from the plate – he threw them to the floor, together with that long and magnificent black hair that looked as though it was from his uncle's head, and then with his shoe he smeared the cakes onto the floor. Jaglika was beside herself with horror at this

(this was her second boza, which she ordered after the lemonade: oh, good grief!), while Uncle F jumped up and led Danilo outside, transporting him through the air by his left ear; Uncle K (who was the cause of the entire scandal) asked the proprietor in a very proper way not to be angry 'at this impudence – the kid's going to get what he deserves', and then he paid him for the pastries we ate, and the cake on the floor, and the mess that'd been made, and then all three of us, Jaglika and he and I, went outside; three or four meters away, Uncle F was giving Danilo a thrashing. Jaglika said: 'He deserves it. This is exactly what he deserves.' Uncle K lit up another *Drina* (from Sarajevo), turned his head the other way, and whistled nonchalantly – what a lack of feeling! Then I, angry to the point of danger, went up to Uncle F and, with all the force I could muster, I kicked him in the shin with the pointed toe of my polished, hard-soled shoe, the left one. Uncle F did not seem to notice, or maybe he didn't feel it, the blow I mean – and he continued beating Danilo fervently and methodically; I struck again, this time in the other leg, and then Uncle F left Danilo alone (such had been my goal); but his next gesture exceeded all my expectations, or to be more precise, it shocked me: he smacked me across the face, so fast (the first slap in my life – is this happening to me, and isn't it always like that?) and so hard, that I burst out crying that same instant. Jaglika said: 'Dear God, these children – it's like they're little demons!' and she crossed herself. Uncle F then announced that the excursion to Topčider was cancelled, and that we were returning to Svetosavska Street, and when, I was under the impression we were all on the way back to our street, I saw the three of them, Jaglika and her two sons, F the older one, and K the fatter younger one, as they disappeared down the street the other way. To Danilo I said, through my sobs: 'It's all your fault. What're we going to tell Marina?' But Danilo was happy, and quiet, as if he had not just had the stuffing knocked out of him by Uncle F, and he replied: 'I really wanna do it. Let's go across the street, Lida, into that little park!' We didn't get back till evening, after having acquired some stamps in the park in exchange for all the marbles we owned, which were a rarity in those days (and which Uncle K brought us from somewhere) …

XI

But who could Vespasian be?! That fancy-pants from the ninth floor! No, that skunk with his red tie and polished shoes and the beret – all right, he hardly knows how to write; once, recently, as I recall, when he rang my doorbell frantically, he was looking for the landlord, and he copied my name like an illiterate onto a duplicated set of instructions and at the bottom he asked for my signature – 'right here you go, where my finger is, and I'm informing you that you'll be fined if you don't buy the radioactivity kit… ', no, it wasn't him, that much is clear as a bell at least. Maybe that mangy old goose down there, from the fourth floor, that bug-eyed cry-baby with the big droopy ass. Who's always bemoaning, through snot and tears, the way everyone has abandoned her, husband, mother, son, daughter, her friend, and how it's unbearable to be by herself and how she doesn't know what to do, or what the hell is the best way to alleviate these torments. No, no… not her, it's not her either, she is, anyway, uneducated, she is, after all, a pure autodidact in life, but who isn't! Vespasian must be, for God's sake – he simply must be a soppy female who's playing a male:

Dear Lidia,

It's simply fantastic that you're hearing me out about this; my wife, or, as the wretches say in the obituaries, my 'spouse', thought up the following fake theory about 'emotions' – she puts it like this,

and she has in mind falling in love (which could also be in quota-
tion marks, at least in her case, because when it comes to this, she's
an embarrassing flop), and so: various affairs, and not to mention
adventures (of both body and spirit) cannot be explained with
reference to blood pressure, high or low, or barometric pressure,
or stomach (midsection) complaints or other corporal-spiritual
difficulties; seeing as how all efforts, she maintains, in that direction result in big fat zeros, she came up with a charming (she says:
logically admissible) revision (in point of fact the outline of a
revision of some medical concepts, and systems and taxonomies –
things built on those concepts; and all of this, she says, is aimed at
regrouping certain phenomena associated with the 'emotionality'
of human beings, at redefining them and labelling them according to the following classes: erythrocytes and leukocytes, in other
words, in accordance with the Latin. Erythrocytes and leukocytes
actually comprise the following groupings (with new names, to
be sure): 1. Purplish bloody grains – the colour of cornflowers,
found in some meadows in the month of June. (To my remark
that cornflowers, always and everywhere, at any time of year are,
if one looks at them properly, yellow, she responded, if you can
imagine, Lidia: 'The adequateness of perceptions and the objective
characteristics of the thing are of no consequence here.') 2. Blue
bloody grains (cornflower again). 3. Very light red (cornflower).
4. Dark red, the darkest of all (cornflower). 5. Moonlight-white
and 6. Greyish white.

The sub-groups of these groupings would be, in regard to colour
and other things, artificially acquired nuances: ground, chopped,
crumbled, dyed, all of cornflower. Therefore, this grouping would
correspond to the so-called erythrocytes. The other grouping (corresponding to leukocytes) would be the colour of early

chrysanthemums in several combinations: reddish white, pinkish grey, orangish green, and so forth. My wife, she says I can check and see how little connection all these have to flowers at the florists' shops in the city, and how conservative they all are and how monotonous. The first set is for the most part inalterable (I told her that's not possible: for the most part; that she would have to decide, for the sake of theoretical consistency: either it's changeable, or it's not!) and the striking presence of certain combinations in which there appeared in the second grouping shades of violet (an unwholesome mixing of white and bloody red grains in some months, even in certain moments – especially then, it will indicate the physiological proclivity to 'emotional outbursts', without the possibility of defence (these are the so-called leukocytes that are – in the customary medical definition – blocked, as if they do not exist). The necessary and natural consequences of such outbursts will be an appearance of the colour blue, cornflower blue, of course. Lidia, such absurdities – and more: speaking again of flowers and the components of blood, my wife says: a third group (thrombocytes in the customary medical sense) is comprised of the colours of roses: you can direct your inquiries to the independent growers (of whom, supposedly, there are enough to populate a metropolis) who by means of cross-breeding obtain, it would seem, very frequently for their roses, greyish-black and also the colour of caraway seeds, and every rose (with those novel nuances) bears the name of a famous person somewhere in the world, dead or alive, it doesn't matter, for instance: the Elizabeth Taylor, Gandhi, Churchill, and Pelé roses. So now, Lidia, why am I telling you this, why am I unloading all this onto you? What nonsense! My wife spent her whole pay cheque, and half my monthly pension, on a handful of books and other things: all of the existing editions of that book, I'm sure you know it, Lidia, it's called *Flowers in Your Home*. All the editions of an anatomy textbook, for students in med school, the first revised edition, the expanded edition, the tenth reworked edition. A few treatises on disintegration (a private publication by some private, unknown individuals). Amongst these is one other book, not uninteresting, entitled: *How to Prepare for Death Without Procrastination!* And in this book there are photos of various machines and devices, but also a completely faithful image of my wheelchair – I even think it's the same brand. Lidia, she has also purchased, for cash, off the top of her head, all the encyclopaedias, even the military ones, plus an easel, together with oil paints. She never took the time to explain this extravagance to me, especially the textbooks for medical students and the painting supplies, except insofar as she told me, as I was writing you: 'You get to hear the basic idea, just so you don't rack your brains about it, and so you don't give yourself an ulcer thinking we won't have anything to eat this month.' Seriously, Lidia, could you lend me a little money? She also said: 'This is a doubling of points, you understand, this inclusion of you in my intentions, but especially in my life, d'you see?' Then she scarpered, and slammed the door (quite the regular gesture, she loves it so much) and shouted: 'Mind your own business, you old fogey!'. But I'm not that old. I just look like I am. The following day, she announced, solemnly (what a stupid woman, what a hopelessly stupid woman): 'The link between character and the shape of one's ass is indisputable.' I told her that that was nothing new at all, that all sorts of rogues, but also honourable people on the various continents, had taken up the issue of such 'links', and she replied that various people and various times were a pain in her ass, and she had nothing but contempt for my doubt, she said, and that was heartfelt, and anyway she intended to amuse herself with this 'link' all the more intensely, much more intensely than anyone had ever done before, or more than they had occupied themselves with it, and that I was going to be her first example, and afterwards she went on to say that I was to be included in any case – that was a correction of course; other than that, she was already writing about it, and about that first part, those colours, and 'I'm doing fine, out of spite towards you', and now, Lidia, you can see that she has completely lost her mind, and you can see, Lidia, what a truly vexing nincompoop I live with. I know, Lidia, I just know, besides which I feel, that you are a much more intelligent woman than this old biddy, and incidentally that wouldn't be hard …

Goodbye, my sweet little Lidia.

What rubbish! Vespasian is a tiresome and persistent bullshit artist, really, and he doesn't even know it.

XII

'If the world did not exist, and had never existed ... then there really would not be any isolated people, for there would be nothing from which one could be isolated ...'

(L.K. N.K.)

1.

Milena, as always, with her feet planted wide apart, and with one red, chapped hand on the handle of the door leading to the outside: 'But listen, Lida, it should not have been like that. You know that thing about how everything has to be done twice, and Danilo should have given that bus conductor another slap, and then when, for example, the first one gets erased, there's only one remaining, I remember that, and so then could a third, you get my meaning, Lidka, then a third could have its uses, so like, you understand, Lidka – it remained unspecified, somehow without cause or motivation, Lidka ... Say, Lidka, did you know I got hired ... totally dumb thing to do ... I'm replacing a woman who's pregnant in the accounting department, you understand, such bullshit, Lidka, the expenses for the hospital, the one over in Banjica, I mean, I was telling you about it yesterday, I don't want to repeat myself, how can I recall, how can I always remember whether something started yesterday or some other day, and what's the harm of repeating myself around you… but get this, Lida, yesterday, no, the day before yesterday, this guy Ivan came into the room where I work. OK, maybe it wasn't Ivan… so, like, who's Ivan? Listen up, Lida, Ivan's a patient, he broke his arm badly, here, like this, and what's more he's deaf and dumb, d'you know what I mean, Lida, and mentally… neglected… so listen up, Lida, he came in all slobbering and barefoot, but all smiles, you know, Lida, and I'd just been there like a day or two… I slept with him, just locked the ol' door… so, okay, Lidia, why is that so terrible? So what if a mentally ill person has normal needs, and if you could have seen his transfigured, smiling, narrow little face, never before in my life have I seen a smile such as that, do you understand, Lidia… and get this part – when I asked him how old he was, he showed me on his fingers, like this… four fingers… there's no way he's forty, and he still looks like a boy, laughing and drooling and afterwards he got all his slobber wiped away, Lida… his insanely handsome face in my skirt and those eyes, totally calm and round like a slaughtered lamb's, Lida, covered with a film of some sort… He didn't want to give me the key, he hid it in his slipper, and oh, what he was like afterwards, you know, that goofy expression that he had on his face – when I ordered him, flat-out commanded him to give me his key… and okay, Lida… what's so bad about that… why is it crazy, you don't understand anything, nothing at all. Come on, Lida, could you make me some coffee… and where's Danilo?'

The first time was just like the later ones: calisthenics, theatrical gestures, exercises in fact – carried out with great skill. First of all, Milena, always, just like always, relates her latest insane amorous experience, and it's the same seduction technique: if I thought of someone's neck, then it was Milena's; somebody's body or face, then it was Milena's; right away she could tell when I was looking at her and when Danilo was doing it the exact same way: she turned into a supple, tall, white Milena, in Danilo's eyes and in mine. In whatever she was doing, the line of her neck was twice as long and radiant as usual; she knew all about how to do that dazzling trick with her neck, with its whiteness and its gleam. But I never grasped why she had such need for the bizarre stories in that whole game of hers! The extent to which it was some kind of repressed need of hers, perhaps, and beyond all calculation, I was not able to discern – that is to say, what kind of need it was.

The narrow, gleamingly smooth and slick surface of Milena's body (the blade of a knife that I see on her belly, leaning against her navel), while we are falling over each other, and Danilo timidly, or conspiratorially, knocks lightly on the door and walks in, pauses in embarrassment for a moment, goes out, and then comes back in, angry. He screams; he howls.

It's always the same technique of seduction; the only part that changes are the degrees of success: touching (walking the beam), together with a focus on the 'inside' – that's what Milena says; every touch, every onset of a touch has to be quiet and slow – drawn out; and then: the skin on her calves and just a little above them, it feels best with only certain parts of your hand, and you have to know exactly which ones; at which angle and under which fingers (it's never all of them) right at first, and which fingers later; the offset of her waist, at the base of her back only comes after touching the recess of her neck, behind the occipital bone and a bit below it, and with the tips of her fingers carefully, and completely tremendously slowly, like when you touch the edge of a piece of unworked glass, the line of her backbone.

Milena did not hide her superiority, and she said: 'Lidia, you're like those miserable guys with whom everything is over before you can blink twice, or at most three times – before you start.'

Aside from that, which is definitely not without significance, Milena also possessed the same indentations and angles, the high line of her derrière, like looking at a competition gymnast from the side; handstand, risky moves several times over: rotations around herself and others. I have no doubt that our relationship was like this: Milena, who gathers polyps, and me, a polyp or a jellyfish, although, if it occasionally looked as though Milena were the polyp and I was the polyp gatherer – that was merely sleight of hand, on account of the radiance of Milena's skin and all the other stuff hidden beneath it. And with regard to that, it does show how often it is possible to come out successful in many things while being guided by base motives.

2.

Jaglika settled her accounts, in a whisper, for days on end, at times with God (whom she believed to be an omnipotent and perfect being), and at other times with the devil: she never ceased holding conversations with the one and the other: 'I never did anything to hurt anyone and I always paid back my debts', and Danilo laughed while bustling around her, teasing her by hiding first her cane, and then her glasses, and then her newspaper, but there was no point: Jaglika had ceased looking for her spectacles, her paper, her cane, or anything else. She slept little, ate nothing at all really, and demanded, straight-out demanded, to go home. Sometimes she called Danilo by our father's name, she mixed up Marina's name with that of her own sister, and as for me, she didn't address me at all except with: her. Or: this one. Which was the same thing.

3.

The whole town was under siege (this is not a reference to Camus); Jaglika is to my left; she has a white kerchief on her head, edged in silver and gold thread. I'm helping her walk, and she's grumbling about how all I want to do is send her sprawling (I'm just waiting for the right opportunity) down into an empty lot (she means the stairs leading up to the fortress of Kalemegdan). All around – (in front of, and behind, Jaglika's eyes and mine, but not to the sides), there's an unusual army, with the same white kerchiefs over their yellow plastic helmets. Convoys of food are rolling past, like well-supplied supermarkets. Rain is falling; the most conventional rain; after a few steps – which the two of us took with much greater effort than usual (Jaglika's entire weight hung on the left side of my body) – we ran into Marina, who was weaving from side to side, and almost falling, drunk as she was; her husband was walking along a step and a half behind her, stiffly, blindly, in actuality he was indifferent. From an alley nearby Danilo burst forth – he was chasing a woman who was pretty but older than his mother, Marina, and he was calling out: 'Mother!' They passed us, Danilo and the woman; I called out to her, as they moved by, 'Good day, ma'am, how are things?' I make a random stop at a roadside stand (a glass-walled grocery store, separated from the food convoy). I buy Jaglika two meat pies. Jaglika was always insufferable when she was seriously hungry; later on she announces that she's tired and I take her in my arms (she's big, and just like a foetus). We ascend a set of steep, twisting stairs, up we go, to the fortress, and we cross the two bridges, with Jaglika saying the whole time: 'Don't you go and accidentally drop me … Don't slip and fall, Lidia, for God's sake,' and she crossed herself, both ways, one after the other

(Jaglika had, since time immemorial, and I know this for a fact, wanted to reconcile her father and mother, with one church in her left pocket, Catholic – and the other church, the Orthodox, in her right pocket – that was her father's). And then: off we went.

I dreamt all this one night, after Danilo slapped the conductor in the bus, or after Danilo's crying. Same thing. But it was cold comfort to Jaglika to think that God created the world for his own glory, out of deeply felt isolation, and that he makes up for this lack of modesty with sincerity, generously, abundantly – as Kolakowski thought. And so, ultimately, it was not difficult to conclude that her isolation (Jaglika is dying) could definitely not be any bigger than God's, at that time when he was considering (and when he was not yet thinking it through – much earlier than that, before everything) creating the world for his own glory.

And what did I have to offer the dying Jaglika! Like water to a thirsty dog! Aside from inconsequential stories about God's isolation! Or, in the same vein, minor relics from nearby churches, and from that self-serve market in the neighbouring street: do I ask her whether she wants, along with the candles and the other stuff, whether she wants a gleaming brass Catholic Jesus? Or should it be a wooden Orthodox one – that very modest Eastern-rite kind? Which side are you on, mother's or father's? Or, perhaps, she would like (I assume she's a sensible old lady) a plastic one, a life-sized Jesus, if, and this is not out of the question, at the moment of decision her little being is overcome by fear and thinks: a plastic, life-sized Jesus is blasphemy, a shameful fabrication, but with wood you're always safe: natural material; with brass even more so: durable material, radiant to the max.

XIII

It was hard for me to grasp, even late in the process; at any rate this was exactly what suits my mind: the same things happened to Danilo and me; we loved the same faces, all the same ones, including our own; there was, however, in everything just one itsy-bitsy difference: Danilo acted, he thought about these things, these people, but I shrewdly (cunning is a distinction of the stupid) took up the role of a non-existent person who does not think about these things, who doesn't act, and is narrow-minded and scorns these things and these faces. I poured forth a torrent of insulting words, curses, and everything I could onto Danilo's otherwise superior being, at his otherwise more beautiful face; and no matter how much the tide of insolence and imagination grew, I grew correspondingly crueller. More and more – for Danilo's beautiful face continued to be beautiful and calm …

Never, not for one instant, did I believe even a single one of the words with which I usually pushed back at Danilo's daydreams, at Danilo's deliberate tomfoolery; but I spoke with authority, with my mouth full, clear-eyed and with my hands loose at my side; although with my palms slightly turned out, too; like a self-assured person who is unaware that she's uttering the wickedest lies that are both as heavy as a ton of stone dropped onto someone's head and as sharp as a metal blade used to slice, in a thin line, precisely, the throat of a lamb or a human being. When Danilo would say:

'Lidia, I had another dream about long, narrow hallways. The way they make you dizzy with their curving and twisting. (I felt like I needed to vomit.) And it made me want to vomit, Lidia!' – I would slip him a lie, like a piece of chocolate in a scrunched-up hand. Actually I would slap it onto his confused face and smear it in: 'Don't be a drag, Danilo. Other people have dreams, too, and they don't make a big fuss about them. Stop thinking only about yourself. Other people – ' And *ad infinitum* about those 'other people'.

To all appearances this thing about 'other people' seemed like a harmless fabrication. When he asked, the way all children do: 'Lidia, are you sure, really really sure, that there's nothing for me to be scared of?' I would also tell him a story about the other people who aren't afraid, while I myself wondered, really, what he had to be afraid of.

I too, however, had my bus incident, my faux pas in a bus. Danilo had been in a crowd, in the throngs of people, other people; he had never been afraid of the extreme proximity of human bodies, and of lousy human smells, menstrual, ammoniac, faecal, urinary... Therefore that thing between him and the female conductor could take place right there in the presence of 'other people'. In situations like that, all I have are the instincts of a frightened dog; I had always been afraid of those sweaty, anonymous packs of flesh who jostle me from behind and press against my back, against my pelvis my stomach my head. Although other people are just a deftly prepared illusion, I did truly fear that they would gouge out my eye, like on a slaughtered lamb, that they would spit in my mouth, down my throat, like in a public urinal, spilling their stinky syphilitic semen down my leg, the way a dog pisses against a tree...

Because of all that, I only rode buses that were almost empty; that time, when my incident happened, there were barely even ten of them there, other people, in the bus. Next to the entrance door, a girl was standing with her back to me; I could not see her face; in fact, I couldn't see anything save her tall, elongated figure and the small, round, perfectly round butt in her pants; their eyes, like mine, were glued to the fabric of her pants, but I alone reached out for it, with my hand – I think I wanted to verify one very simple thing: whether the curve of that perfect ass differed under my fingertips from the same lines and same ass that people had before their eyes – mine and those of the others. And as soon as I touched it, everyone on the bus – all of a sudden there were a thousand of them – began to croak, maliciously: 'Shame on you!' and 'Throw her off the bus!' and 'Pervert' and 'Yuck, a lesbian!' but I don't think the young woman even felt my touch. Ultimately, that rear-end, round and petite, had no connection of any kind to the girl's body, and not to mine, either.

When I told Milena about this, she waved it off, laughed at me, and said: 'Oh, get real, Lida! We both know that the satiny little ass in the bus is made of meat. Tender or chewy, it's all the same!'

XIV

Our friend Milena only came over so she wouldn't have to be alone when she talked to herself. Later I realized that this wasn't self-infatuation, nor anything along those lines; now I can even affirm, although it doesn't do anybody much good now, that it was Danilo who first sensed the seriousness of Milena's isolation. Milena's ardent penchant for humiliation (never once did I try to hit her; several times I pinched her (blue streaks remained); I told her everything that a person can say to herself, to another person, to no one, everything that can be thought up, imagined, and then forgotten) proved to be a grave matter. After all, only out of a sense of seriousness is it possible to permit the things that Milena permitted.

The one person who felt repentant was me, always me; Milena was constantly sombre; Danilo worried, and sometimes he cried.

I fantasized that it would be possible to spend the rest of one's life without moving: Milena and I, as a double static figure in Svetosavska Street; Milena with her legs hooked – her hips around my neck, and her head between my legs – never-ending wetness, and all around – the moving world: Danilo and his bug-eyed Marko, whispering, prodding each other, and walking on tiptoes, going, coming, the both of them peering through all the keyholes; Jaglika and Čeda sending postcards with their regards, walking around the big park at Košutnjak, Little River sticking right by Jaglika's side; my boss issuing various orders, going out to the cinema with his wife, never failing to reflect on the fate of the world in front of the shop window featuring fancy leather goods, and yawning in the library; and Milena and I like stalactites.

Of course, I was not able to avoid ensnaring myself in Milena's serenity; no matter what I did, no matter what I said to her, Milena would always just curl up the corners of her lips, grinning, sneering at me with those gleaming front teeth of hers that were so large, and the big, retracted lower jaw, which she would then pull back even more, always but always repeating: 'Oh for God's sake, Lida!'

And when I slapped her one time, Milena said: 'Oh for God's sake, Lida!' – and she left with a smile on her face. From the balcony I shouted down; I asked her to come back; and she turned around once and grinned again, as if she were waving, but said again: 'For God's sake, Lida!' Creep! I ran to Jaglika; I squeezed onto her lap and cried and kissed the backs of her wizened, gnarled hands, slobbering and whispering into her lap (my head was moored to the bottom of her stomach – and her lap was right there on that itsy-bitsy spot way down low): '*Baba*, may God help us, you and me,' and Jaglika would say, bewildered, 'Get off me, child… Why me? I didn't do anything to anyone. Go on, move over. Move over when I tell you to!'

A Story from Childhood

It was in the coastal town of Umag, where we were spending our summer vacation for the second time – precisely there, and because of that – and Danilo and I were still little; Marina was laughing and sunbathing with this dark-haired guy. Uncle K was hanging around. In the evening the three of them, Uncle K, Marina, and the swarthy guy from the beach, left us to sleep; they headed out to a nearby tavern. After Danilo and I determined that there was no danger of their swift return, we stole out of the house; Danilo put on his bathing trunks and a thick sweater; I had on pyjama bottoms and a t-shirt; we went down to the beach – it was a few hundred meters away; other than that I just had a rubber band on my head; my hair was tangled and damp – tied up in a rubber band (after the day's swimming) – Marina didn't even like (she simply hated to have to mess with my hair, in the evenings) to touch my head, my hair – and therefore I always went to bed with my hair uncombed. When we got down there, to the beach, I told Danilo – whom I had carried on my back from the halfway point (he was complaining that his legs ached an awful lot) – how nice it would be if we could also take a swim – and I added that that's why we had come out of the house in the dark. I assured him that there was absolutely no reason to be afraid, since I had in my mouth an unusually long piece of twine – which we would use to tie ourselves to one of the boats so that we wouldn't be lost to the waters, or to the darkness. Danilo was still on my back; I set him down, on the sand, and he started crying that very instant – he was always crying – both when he should be crying and when he shouldn't; I sat down beside him and begin withdrawing the twine from my mouth; it was astonishingly long – I pulled it out length by length or (at those places where it was tied) knot by knot, and it seemed like it had dropped deep down my throat – I wasn't anywhere near getting to the end of it out; and when I got sick, I vomited up the final little knot and all my food, a heap of food – which had been stewing in my stomach for days; Danilo never let up crying; damn brat, it's amazing how strong he is! I got into the water a moment later, ignoring Danilo (he was shrieking by now, and it sounded like animals from out of the darkness were ripping him into shreds of varying sizes) and without the twine. I swam around a little bit and then quickly came back out; Danilo only grudgingly agreed to give me the sweater – only when I promised to carry him all the way back. By the time we were a few steps away from the house, Danilo had already fallen asleep; the three of them: Marina, the dark-haired guy and Uncle K were waiting with cudgels in their hands; Danilo didn't experience the terrible judgement himself, the holy trinity: the fury of this midnight trio descended with full force on my small weak back, without mercy, and all of it ostensibly for this reason: 'We were worried to death here.'

XV

'At the foot of the city, in the time of King Ateas, a ten-story slaugh-
terhouse was erected; not a single animal was sacred; especially not
dogs; later this ornate structure was converted into a storehouse for
traditional weapons from prehistory (arrows, spears, various daggers
with short handles), and others.'

(P. I. S. a)

For the first five, or even six, years of his life, Danilo would chase
birds down every street in the city; in Knez Mihailova, he would
charge into a peaceful flock of pigeons, white ones and grey ones,
and in a moment's time he would have dispersed all of them; the
people out for a Sunday stroll, casting crumbs with such ludicrous
care and all their Sunday refinement, taking pictures of themselves,
some of them anyway, got mad as hornets. To whom were they
shouting, without any trace of refinement, all of a sudden: 'Watch
out for the little monster! He belongs in an institution, not on
the street…' Doubtless they thought that the so-called home for
delinquent children, and that street with the pigeons, formed
the apotheosis of those little starched Sunday dresses, the white
petticoats, of their children, the polished booties, and the equally
starchy grown-up smiles; and in their pockets, on Sundays, they
always had handfuls of crumbled food for the birds, right there
across the street from the American Reading Room. For a full

five, or six (no one knows precisely), years of his life, Danilo drew birds in the corridors of our building on Svetosavska, in improbably resistant colours; none of the caretaker's silly efforts at daubing paint over them over the next six years bore fruit: the birds, on every floor, and on every standing wall, they could be seen, and some of them were still quite distinct, despite layers of paint. 'The building is intolerably grubby,' said all the folks who lived in Svetosavska. For those first five or six years of his life, Danilo also left birds behind on sheets of paper, on newspapers, on wardrobes, tiles, and doors … Every day Jaglika would throw away countless clutches of bird-paper, and she believed quite firmly that this was a divine punishment. She crossed herself both ways, just to be on the safe side – propitiating first one God and then the other. Right to left, and then again: left to right. When Danilo started school, the bird thing stopped; at last, the Sunday strollers could relax, and they would never again see 'that holy terror running like a madman into the birds on the pavement, waving his arms and pretending to shoot them … ' The building council, too: at last the great horrors on our walls of Svetosavska Street were covered by an extraordinarily thick layer of paint.

Danilo, however, started to stutter; he stuttered more and more, and turned red and cried, and would cry again; Marina took him once to see this famous man who knew his way around such things – there weren't any results to speak of but I guess it was worth it – but maybe it was for another reason, too, so that the dude who was famous for children's tribulations would become one of the first of Marina's lovers and would almost never leave our house on Svetosavska. Jaglika made the sign of the cross in amazement with both her left hand and her right and she mentioned a church – to which she that very minute needed to take Danilo.

Not once did I hear her say, in that croaking way of hers (because of her dentures which were loose and unstable): 'He is to blame for everything… That's easy as can be, and anybody could do it… It's like yanking off someone's ponytail, and staring wide-eyed but leaving the others. You can't do that. You just can't…'

It took several long years, but I came to know the overall meaning, and finally the content, of these things that Jaglika repeated. Her whisperings. Uncle K mentioned to me briefly, one day when I was seventeen (he had dropped by for a coffee), it was in the morning, a half hour before I was supposed to head to school: 'Your father strung himself up in prison when you were four years old. Danilo was younger; they had arrested him several days before, for some kind of check; in those days tons of people were arrested for routine checks, but he turned out to be a coward, a major coward. He had slipped away from the special police all during the war, and afterwards, but then he hanged himself like the big pussy that he was.'

Before she left for Ljubljana, to her relatives – that was in the same year that Marina had brought that guy home to Svetosavska – Jaglika told Danilo, in the same moment that he, for Lord knows what reason, mentioned our father's family: 'You poor fellow, can't you see that they've all disappeared? Like bitches in heat they raised their tails and off they went… ' But Danilo, not comprehending how hard-headed Jaglika was, said: 'But, *Baba*, they aren't alive, you know? They're all long since dead.'

'The hell they aren't. They were alive, and while they were alive they never thought of you two, they never came to see Lidia or you since you were both bastards, and they never gave you anything… ' That was Jaglika's response, delivered with a full dose of malice, as if the fact that no one had ever given us anything comprised everything; when Danilo, forgetting for a second about Jaglika's shopkeeper mentality and past, tried to explain to her how none of them, but none of them, had had an easy time of it, she jumped all over him. Enraged, she screamed at him: 'Shut up! Shut up about this! Things weren't easy for them, but were they easy for us? I know that nest of vipers quite well, sons of bitches… Your father would've been exactly like them if he'd stayed around by some miracle… You have nothing to regret.' After this, Danilo hit *Baba* with a pair of kitchen tongs; Jaglika raised hell, cursed, threatened us, and, in the end, locked herself in her room; she remained angry for precisely two days; she got her things in order, supposedly so she could return to Ljubljana – 'no one insults me there or screws with me.' On the third day, Jaglika erased from her heart every bit of anger, like an eraser on paper, and soon one could hear this around the house: 'Oh, where's my little Danilo, my sweetie, my little chick-a-dee, granny's favourite, her little man, the pride and joy of his granny…'

XVI

Milena's body, velvety, smooth, and warm; no, it's her skin; it's quite possible that it's a matter of my imagination; which nevertheless is also warm, radiant, and smooth. The colour of her slip (it encircled her legs like a silk army parachute – that kind that the hippie kids make dresses, skirts, and other stuff out of) was ivory; ivory and jade, green and yellow mixed, or so it looks from here in bed: the slip on the floor and Milena naked.

Milena steps out of her big army umbrella-slip, and lifts the blanket on my bed: 'But you're still dressed, Lida… Why all the stalling!!' I got naked in a hurry then; but I left on my underwear, green – it belonged to Milena's long and impatient fingers; I also left on my tank-top, blue with green shoulder straps – now that belongs, too, to Milena's ready nervous fingers; it goes unceremoniously over my head. Rapidly, Milena's mouth, all of it, on my sex, all of it. I think about my own skin, rough, darkened by numerous illnesses, (Milena seldom skipped a chance to mention the unbelievable whiteness and softness of her skin, over against mine, which was hard, rough, and nearly black; she would say, for instance, 'easy-to-light charcoal and quality-controlled [brilliant white] rational lust, nothing worse than that, right Lida?'), and I think about Tsvetaeva's neck in Dagestan, after she squeezed it through the noose, bewildered and moving fast (but who would've stopped her?!), immediately, that same instant (only nobody saw this) – her neck turned jade and ivory, yellow and green like Milena's skin and unyielding, unyielding like mine. I knew that Milena and Jaglika don't understand these things; I know that it's not as easy as falling off a log; whether, for example, Mihailo, my father, or Tsvetaeva, no matter who, but let's say Mihailo anyway, 'that man' from the many years of Jaglika's whisperings around the house (Milena's teeth, then tongue, then teeth again, and then just her lips all over my dimpled thighs; and the room, by the way, is unheated), whether he, the moment before his legs bucked and buckled – since he hanged himself from the radiator – whether he thought about the world, about the skin he was abandoning, or whether his field of vision was completely restricted: how to pull this off as fast as possible: tighten the belt, stick his head through, closing his eyes first – no one should see the whites of those eyes, of course, since people love to say, and even Jaglika said it: 'It just looks like he's asleep' – such a crock of shit, like this too: 'He's so handsome it looks like he's only sleeping.' That is so fucked up for Christ's Sake. What does Milena know, white Milena, about whether Mihailo or Tsvetaeva, whoever, looped his or her head through the noose rapidly and skilfully, or was mystified and scared, embarrassed at the outset, more and more certain as the pace picked up, and then slow for the pleasure of it, disgusted perhaps, feeling repulsive the whole time, or was it the way it is under a pillow or into the gorge? Maybe Mihailo's neck was just like Milena's now: tensed-extended with no end of sinews, veins, and bruises. Milena came and put her mouth on mine; Milena brushes her teeth twenty times a day and constantly says: 'You've always got a lake of spit in your mouth, Lida. It's like you don't swallow... for God's *saaake*, Lidia, what do you do with it all?

Learn how to swallow, Lidia. I'm choking over here ... Lidia!'
And shortly thereafter, crossly: 'Why are you gawking at me like
that? I don't know what to do with you.'

In the morning (with her long arms out over the blanket), while
she drank coffee and spilled some (it ran out over her chin) here
and there, Milena didn't talk about dreams as some people do,
or as all people do – it was the same every morning, with the
same long arms (all arms are long) out over the blanket, or with
her hands behind her head – so that her elbows jutted out to
the sides, she would finish some mundane thoughts from the
previous evening, or from some night out, talking from morning
till noon – always the same thing, with tiny and inconsequential
changes:

'The most useless thing in the world, no, wait ... the saddest
thing, for real, Lida, is when you are fucking some loser who's
flailing around down there and doesn't know where anything
is in the huge space, you know, it's true, and when a misfit like
that says to you: does it hurt, and maybe you're thinking Lida of
something that won't insult him, you totally just don't want to
offend him with something that will trample the illusion he has
that his cock is big and has stamina and is powerful and clever and
everything it should be but his dick is like a worm, the fucker, and
it makes you want to cry, cry from nausea at his torment, and now
look here ... listen, where does this compassion come from, Lida,
on which everything rests, do you understand Lida, it's on this
compassionate relationship to worms, the worms, Lida, would
croak the moment they knew, Lida, if only they knew they were
worms, in other words, that everything around them is not also
a worm, do you understand, Lida, it's simply impossible.'

'What's impossible?' I ask. Milena sets her empty coffee cup on the floor and says: 'Worms, Lida, worms are impossible… But Lida you got divorced I assume because of that?'

'Because of what?' I ask.

'Because of his worm.'

'No, Milena. It was boring, the way it is with you. It was insufferably boring, do you understand, Milena?'

'That means he left you. He found somebody better. I mean, somebody with softer skin!'

'You don't understand, Milena. There are things under skin level.'

'I know Lidia but what's under the skin shows up on the skin, and skin is important.'

XVII

Vespasian again:

Dear Lidia,

I've been away on a trip and that's why I haven't contacted you for so long. I spent hours at Gundulić Meadows, always keeping my eye on two, or at most three, scenes at once, while my wife carried on nude under the water, in the hotel room, in the bathtub, on the terrace, in a grove of trees, etc. Incidentally, you know, I couldn't do anything, or more precisely, maybe I could have if she'd wanted. But, as you know, my face disgusts her, as do my immobile legs and you know it to be true, Lidia, about this type of revulsion, I don't think you're utterly dissimilar to my wife – I don't mean to sound like I'm saying 'all women are the same,' but close to it you know? As for Gundulić Meadows, I wasn't in a position to see how far I could shoot my load – I've never done that before when I was surrounded by other people, but actually maybe I have, if I consider my wife to be, you know what I mean, consider her as a multitude, as different persons. I sat there for hours, and at some point my wife came to get me – she was returning from the first round of fucking that day, her face red as flame, with wet hair and her face beatific and, Lidia, 'terribly hungry' – and it was all 'let's get a move on, c'mon, I'm starving, I'm dying of hunger' – and then she pushed me towards the City Café.

I had made friends with someone who was half-hippie, half-peasant – he was selling watermelons. You know how they do that, Lidia: first they spit several times into their hands, as if they are using sorcery to heal somebody; then they rub their pooled sputum all over the watermelons – later he explained the reason for that to me: so the watermelons would shine in the sun and in order to get the dust off. 'Why don't you wash them with water, at the fountain,' I asked him. And he, Lidia, so persuasively said it was very complicated to take already unloaded watermelons one by one from the stand to the fountain. After washing them with spit, with one long fingernail (he has two of them, one on each pinkie) he scratches numbers onto the melon's rind. He keeps his money in one of his socks, and he also has two big boots adorning his feet. Somewhere around one o'clock, or one-fifteen, every day, the time comes when he knows exactly how much he has sold and how much he'll still be able to sell by three o'clock, and he cracks open a watermelon (he splits it on the edge of the counter, eats a little, and tosses the rest to the pigeons) and then when we struck up our friendship, he started giving me a piece, too, and I took it – it did not gross me out, Lidia, didn't gross me out in the least, but there's no way for you to understand that. The Eastern and Western tourists, and there were other kinds there surely, they didn't take any notice of how this guy cleaned his watermelons, and he sold so many of them every day that when he left at three or three-fifteen at the latest, he also had to use one of his boots to store part of the money. Until I got to know him, I had been observing hideous scenes for days: female tourists with ghoulish sunglasses and really big noses and totally square derrières who are practically squatting in rows, stubbornly trying with a few scraps of corn to entice the already satiated and disgustingly fat birds, and off to the side, two steps away, stood the stubborn and patient husbands in columns counted off like their wives, with cameras held at the ready; the women and the pigeons, you have no idea, Lidia, the kinds of nightmares I had, every day, every afternoon, and every night, too (except when I was sitting on Gundulić Meadows, I spent a half hour after lunch in the City Café, and all the rest of the time I was asleep); I have not ceased dreaming about those filthy birds and the human heads, the bodies; the repulsive, fattened pigeons as they drilled out my eyes with their beaks, and the human figures suffocated me with their square derrières, with several of them sitting down at the same time on my neck and my face.

But the watermelon guy grinned and giggled whenever he'd relate the adventures he'd supposedly had with the foreign women. I didn't believe a word of what he said; anyway he looked too unpolished, too much so even for that so-called Balkan virility. He'd say about one woman that she could fart loud enough to be heard over on the island of Lokrum, and about another one he'd say her pussy was unbelievably large, but of course he still banged her just fine, it actually fit him, and in general this watermelon guy bragged about himself; I thought my wife would think the same way about this guy, for sure, if he were maybe a little more polished: if he didn't spit into his hands, for instance. But there's no doubt that he didn't do it with her, that is, that she found someone who never did that, because my wife suffers from a certain complex: she only fucks around with so-called intellectuals, even if those brain-iacs of hers are not only impotent but unattractive, pockmarked and whatever, in the first place…

When we came back, everything was the same at before; in the sun there I had forgotten, or it couldn't be seen, I didn't notice, I even thought that she was a beautiful and healthy woman, you really could not see it there: her interior constitution; Lidia, her interior constitution had bolts and screws that were visible and audible in her eyes, in her belly, and especially, especially, Lidia, when she walked – like a mechanical doll; never, actually, do I know what is happening until her 'feelings' – she calls them 'emotions' – start to suffocate, to stink, in intellectualized sentences – she, Lidia, has done nothing but spout bullshit as long as I've known her, and she never ever even gets a squeamish look on her face, on the contrary, everything is mechanically graceful, on her face, Lidia, I know that you won't understand this, because you are most likely very similar to my wife …

Goodbye, sweet little Lidia

I most probably did have one other trait, among all the other ones, that was similar to Vespasian's wife – as if Vespasian's wife was only one characteristic, one distinction, let's say, of one unnecessary man: I was, like her, I presume, obsessively pedantic; I've already said that I signed every one of Vespasian's letters for 'God forbid' (the police), sometimes in this colour and sometimes in that colour of ink, and stacked them up, and then I numbered them here in Roman numerals and there in Arabic ones, and so on; this letter was the one I put on the top of the whole lot of them, contrary to my custom up to then – and I had at that instant the firmest of intentions to find out who Vespasian truly was, but in the next moment something threw me off, which Vespasian did not take into account, nor did he ever dream of it in those night-time and day-time nightmares of his, he didn't take into account, he could not have, even if he is from Rome, that he, by some miraculous happenstance, is the real Vespasian, and this is too great a similarity between him and me, not between his distinction (his wife) and me. He will never grasp this – that it's between him and me. However, the people from the police station 'God forbid', when they get their hands on these letters of Vespasian's, I have no doubt, that they will be exactly as stupid as God requires and commands and will conclude that Vespasian does not exist, and that I am writing these letters to myself, but once more in accordance (again it is a matter of divine harmony) with how those lords from the station 'God forbid' would act: it might turn out to be useful that we, however, lock her up as a security measure for an unspecified period of time, you never know whether instead of writing to herself she might start writing letters to other people, and continue signing them 'Vespasian', we have to, we must, what will people think, et cetera...

But did I not say, and I'm telling you again just in case, that they are the only ones allowed to get things mixed up, or, more precisely, it's only their stupidity that gets to do that.

XVIII

'No, I did not imagine it, Milena. I remember perfectly well how the holes opened up here in the street on Svetosavska, and green dinosaurs started coming out of them, but I didn't, I surely wasn't dreaming, Milena; listen, you've forgotten that you at one point said: "Calm down, Lida, it's all plastic, don't you see," and then you turned to Čeda of Little River who was already waiting, quaking and stooped, and red from your white flesh, yeah, from your white flesh. He was a terrible sight. He was scared just like me. You saw it, Milena, even though you're pretending to be clumsy now, and even if you were pretending to be clumsy then, you did, you saw it, you saw Čeda's fear, and again later, Milena when there was that unnecessary, bad combining thing: Čeda, sweaty and cold, you, and I, although, yeah, with a lot of effort from you, finished, on the floor, like always. You had concocted, even if you say now that you don't remember, a moronic game with pinching, tickling, and dressing up in other people's clothes, something like a masked ball. First I put on Čeda's clothes; then I took them off, and then you put them on, after which Čeda put mine on, and so on, on down the line. You devised the unsavoury ritual whereby everyone needed to appear in everyone else's clothes, without any explanation whatsoever; and then, how do you not recall, how in God's name do you not recall this, Milena, the dumbest thing of all happened: I again lay down on the floor, although that got me all dusty and dirty, and you pressed something, no you didn't do it too hard, something plastic against my throat, like a knife. Čeda was standing off to the side and trembling, and anyhow you were putting on this entire masquerade for his benefit; Čeda's fright amused you, when he, after you told him: "This is gentle, bring on the real one," he, Čeda, still quivering, obeyed and brought it, mortified by fear. You were furious. I got up off the floor. Everything went wrong all at once. Čeda breathed a sigh of relief, even if he was also smiling, and you saw it, I knooow, Milena, that you saw it, even if you deny it now, even if you're continuing to play dumb, God, such a pile of… You totally know that's how it was, you and Čeda both… of course it's true that Čeda's never admitted he was scared… but he knows, he remembers too, as do I, how you were getting dressed at the same moment that I was getting up off the floor, and you ordered him to get dressed, too; you were saying, "let's get out of here, Čeda," and he listened to you, of course. You know, Milena, you could do any-thing and everything with Čeda, just like with Danilo. Anything…'

Milena said nothing for several minutes (and that belongs under the rubric of her skills: she devises a lie, or she doesn't devise one, because she already thought it up and is only embellishing, just as calmly as if she were pressing her lips together and then opening her mouth and then encircling it with dark red lipstick) just like she was opening and pursing her lips – a red-rimmed hole appears on the white-moon face, and from there gushes forth, as from a septic tank: 'Listen, pay attention now, Lidia… There are people who go through doors face-first, who wait for the doors to open for them, and then there are those who sneak in sideways alongside you, past you, edge-wise, and then the people who take a full step backwards after they ring the doorbell and who wait for you to ask them several times to "come on inside", and why don't you go in, well, go on, and be careful now, and a moment ago when you rang, you were simply waiting, with your fear there somewhere, you understand, I could not leave you, and then Čeda didn't get scared and you did, then and now, listen Lidia, you stood there a moment ago like a soldier no like a child you know that child-soldier do you remember the child-toy, the wooden soldier and now I knew listen Lidia I knew about that fear over there somewhere although you were calm do you understand Lidia compleeetely calm, good Lord, the kind of fear that was protruding you know just flat-out sticking out, gushing out all over your disgusting, dumb-ass face and I had to get away from you, although I could have closed the door on you, do you see, Lidia, I had to leave you... and what is it you want now, Lidia, you fabricated all of this, Čeda's fear, then, my power over Čeda, he didn't obey me, do you understand, Lidia, you did, Lidia, you forgot, Čeda said: "Let's go." It wasn't me, I listened to him, it was unbearable, Čeda remembered first, he just found his bearings in the miracle of your imaginings, you were talking nonsense, and, Lidia, you distorted everything, you've forgotten that you ran naked out of the kitchen with a knife, without any passion in you whatsoever, it is true, but still it was terrifying, and you said: "Come on now, let's play, let's try this out," d'you understand, even though the whole time it was you, you were the one who was scared, you were scared to the point of being debilitated, listen, Lidia, like now, too, and Čeda was, and you're forgetting this, he was more than anything delighted and peaceful, I mean, he was glad, do you understand, Lidia, isn't it obvious to you, Lidia... What the hell, *Lidiaaa*, why did you come why did you call me do you think I don't know about your deceits, it's my fault about Danilo, I did this and that with Danilo, but the thing with Čeda was your idea, yours, you've forgotten, you had said: "oh, why nooot, Milena, what's wrong with that, he's handy," you arrange all these idiocies as you see fit, I put up with all of it, your random schizoid variations on a theme, and Čeda, and this, and that, later you cook up the notion that Danilo was in love with me, but he wasn't and he hadn't been, you know, can you see this Lidia, he never was… it was important for you to think so, you dragged him into all this, you were constantly intriguing, just wouldn't ever stop I never had any relationship with him listen Lidia you know this… you know it's true about Danilo, Lidia…'

XIX

I've always thought that plaits, pigtails, or even a pony-tail – with that bouncy curvy part at the end – need to be at least half as thick as one of Jaglika's legs. The obsessions with Jaglika's legs, which I believe belonged to my childhood (to the real one or the made-up one, it didn't matter), actually never left me, not for a moment, so to speak. When Milena's mother passed away, last month, in the oncology unit in a really big room with fifty other people (where by the way there were four times as many cockroaches, so, for every dying person four of them, therefore two hundred of those tough black things were there to help the moribunds acclimatize to their future); I went to visit her (the things we do!) wearing a red cap with a small brim – similar to those caps in grotesque little stories – from our universal and mutual childhood schooling, and with one thick plait – I hung down the back of my neck and head. The cap and the plait made me feel safe; it seemed to me (I was almost sure of it) that, instead of my own two legs, I had both of Jaglika's, big, thick, and firm, and it wasn't just a heavy plait on my head, along with that red cap. There's no doubt that the excursion was totally just for show. Before then I had met Milena's mother a grand total of once in my life. Then, that time in the hospital was the second time. I'm not completely certain, however, that there didn't exist something in connection with Milena, some need, however incon-venient it was at that moment. And that cap and the plait – the great obsession of my childhood was, however, a falsely interpreted manifestation, falsely interpreted as a manifestation: Milena, seeing (after coming into the room ten minutes behind me) that I was seated at the head of her mother's bed, quietly summoned me to go out, and then, in the corridor there, in front of that closed door to the room for dying patients, she said, half audibly through clenched teeth: 'Get lost, you scumbag.'

Much later, a person told me, a person who is completely irrelevant, that she heard from Milena that her mother, at the moment (and this could have been that very day on which I'd gone there with my plait and cap) she was giving up her soul, actually in the instant before she gave up Milena and left her all alone in the world, she said, very distinctly, despite the morphine, or maybe because of it: 'a big fat rabbit ran between my legs.'

It's quite possible that these final words are fictitious. That is to say, just garden-variety gossip. It's also quite possible that a sentence reached my ears via that inconsequential person in a distorted form, or that here, inside my head, it got twisted around a hundred times. What's the link between giving up the ghost and a rabbit? I thought: well, maybe it has to do with this: the speed of the departure for heaven is equal to the speed of the imaginary rabbit that ran by you, and the fat part means this and the warm part means that and if it squeezes through your legs it … But the cancer ward, and now Milena's mother, come to think of it, would be the ones to say.

After visiting the cancer ward, that is, Milena's mother, I went to Svetosavska Street. Danilo and Marko Eyepiece were sitting there, drooling over those porno films, foaming at the mouth and tittering. Marko shouted from the door, 'Lidia, hey Lidia, you gotta see the new film, it's fantastic, you'll see why I'm so…' Then the three of us stayed there till morning with a little hashish and a lot of ridiculous movies; at 4 a.m., Marko Rat Eyepiece abruptly started packing up the movies, the screen, changing his glasses as he did so; he crammed everything into one of those indestructible eternal plastic bags, pushing it all in amongst the other delicacies: a John Dewey and a Bergson, then three airline timetables, the remaining bundle of hash, which he didn't want to give us, six pairs of glasses (the seventh was on his face) and somebody's final dissertation – to trade to a student for cash. I followed him out with the bicycle, with Danilo remaining behind, scared: 'Lidia, where are you riding off to when it's all dark like this?' But: 'Not into the dark, Danilo. Just going around the block a few times.' Then it was already past five, and had grown completely light, or six, when totally knackered I pushed the bike down the hallway, carried it up the steps – it wouldn't fit in the lift, I entered our apartment and found completely awake and tear-stained, sweet Jesus, a snot-covered Danilo, good Lord, what, what would Marina do now, she'd caress it, his face, Danilo's beautiful face, which was at the same time her own (the two of them resembled each other), but I couldn't, I can't, I don't know how, I won't do what Marina would. I give my bike a shove and scream: 'Fuck you all to hell…you moron why aren't you sleeping why do you sit around puling your whole fucked-up life away you idiooot get lost!'

XX

'Let's count on a reward at the going market rate, and not according to how much effort we have invested in our work.' (L.K. to N.K.)

Around that time it became a certainty that Milena wasn't going to call or come by. At first I tried my absolute hardest (it wasn't different in the least from a terminal patient who breathes his/her tortuous final breath) to disfigure, deform, warp, shatter, slice up her image in my head, and the rest of whatever else on me, in me, bore a connection to her; and that childish, a priori failure, everything from which I desired to free myself: Milena.

I'd walk into Jaglika's room right after work, straight from the bus, running, and every day I'd ask that dying figure from the doorway, wrapped in her fifteen blankets – in her rocking chair with glasses on the tip of her furrowed, likeable nose, her swollen feet in slippers with black tassels, the same thing:

'Do you love me, grandma?'

'What's that you're saying?' (The first thing to go is the ears, and then it's the eyes and the heart, when you're dying.)

'I was asking … whether you love me?' (I was screaming; you have to push a dying person into talking about love.)

'Why's that? Do you love me?' (This only makes it look like a dying person has a greater need for love than the one who's asking, regardless of the gender in question.)

'But I asked you that, *baba*.' (One should be hard-nosed, avoid pity and other such excesses).

'I love you the exact same amount you love me.' (Someone who's mortally ill needs to be hustled into death.)

'No more and no less. No more or no less, *baba*?'

'Definitely, exactly as much as you love me and not a whit less or a whit more, Lidia, but why are you asking?' (We have to give the moribund another shove!)

'But this isn't like running a shop, d'you know what I mean, grandma?'

'Yep…Uh-huh, yep…' (The conversation of the deaf.)

'But *baba*, you're a business person, and when you die, they're going to ask you over there, God will ask you, what you did. What did you do for those unfortunate souls amongst you, and your answer will help separate the sheep from the goats… *baba*, like a little leech a miserable pawnbroker hissing through your dentures: I was all business, always thinking of deals, what else could I do when my father and husband were merchants.' (Cruelty also has the blessing of Jaglika's God.)

'Go away, you scoundrel…Go over there!' (The dying are always braver than the living.)

Jaglika was overcome by a fit of rage, great rage, unsuited to her aged being (and to a mercantile one, too); she took up her cane every time I mentioned a god or anything else divine, and she tried to hit me. I jeered at her from a safe distance; Jaglika's cane was almost never able to reach the spot where I stood, or sat, or crouched.

'You've been retailing your whole life, *baba*. Do you hear me, *baba*?'

In those days the determination of the one who was living (that was me) to demonstrate at any cost her superiority over the moribund, was mind-bogglingly small, at least as far as Jaglika was concerned, but also in a wider context; no one could forecast when her powers might burst forth – especially when it seemed like all of her reactions, of any type, were absent; all the more reason that her capacities were stunning, like the time she lunged (the immobile Jaglika who lurched forward – really, like in a bad movie) and with precision (concentration) – and without missing a beat or tiring, started brandishing her cane, complete with a copious amount of spitting (it spewed forth like a fountain from her blue-tinged lips) and accompanied by the words: 'Move when I say to, you degenerate hussy, move on over, you bitch...'

The cane, dying Jaglika's cane, caught me right smack-dab in the stomach.

Jaglika never did get over that grocery shop of hers in Nikšić; after it was burned down at the end of the last war, she wept as if everything in it were a living creature, or at least as if Marina were inside. Besides, in 1928, the shop was still running well; she sold things 'at the lowest prices' (for a trifle, as it were). 'Šiht' soap, 'Marseilles' soap, and the brand called 'Vila', petroleum both in crates and in barrels, and semolina, lard, as well as 'Karolina' rice and 'Gigant' and 'Splendor', too, and top-drawer coffees like 'Minas' and 'Rio'. 'Blažo, the teacher, did all his shopping there right up until he died, may God have mercy on his soul,' – Jaglika said. In 1934, she went into bankruptcy; it 'almost put me six feet under, in two more days it would have all been over' – that's how Jaglika recalled the ruin of her shop, like it was the end of a world; and she was right. But then, after two or three years, the grocery owned by

Jaglika and her husband was back on its feet, and you could shop there again 'at the lowest prices in the whole *banovina* region, either for retail or wholesale, no matter which.' So how did life unfold after that point for Jaglika's family, in terms of groceries and dry goods and the rest of it? They grew wealthy, and first they bought up a women's clothing store; they ran ads for sales, as ever with that 'lowest price' thing, in Dubrovnik's *Tribuna* up to 1937 and then in *Slobodna Misao* over the course of 1938 and again in 1940; they got their stock of clothing from a salesman named Šavni, who was from Škofja Loka in Slovenia. Jaglika also used to mention a man named Nikebroker who had some strange connection to their family. In '37 they went several times to the cinema to watch two movies: *Kostja the Shepherd* and *A Kingdom for a Kiss*. But Jaglika said they didn't see the film *The Tsar's Messenger* a single time. Why not? Her uncle's sister, who married an Armenian man in Istanbul, for which Jaglika never forgave her, used to send them various herbs and medicines for their stomachs from there; stomach-ache was a common malady for Jaglika's whole family, including those two brothers of her uncle, the ne'er-do-wells who later, together with Jaglika, ran a small shop in Zagreb, for a year, before the war broke out – they fled without a backwards glance, off to God knows where (Jaglika never wanted to say: where, oh where did those lowlifes scram to?), while she returned to Nikšić. Stefanida, her relative, that was her name, thus ended up dying in Istanbul, but the war was going on, 'otherwise I would've gone to her funeral,' said Jaglika.

'And so, now you have some place to get that magnesium purgative, you'll see, like in the wink of an eye, easy-peasy, I picked it up with the tip end of a knife, you can see how much of it that is, a crumb with a little water or on a dumpling…' Jaglika told me that only I could have the medicine that she 'used to get from Stefanida' back then and take 'after a meal, off the point of a knife-blade' in order to cure my stomach pains.

Of course Jaglika never had any doubt that this was a question of the alchemical capabilities of an Armenian, in collaboration with a big-boned woman with a Byzantine name – a fact also not without importance … No … not with Byzantine eyes, though, but, let's say, Egyptian ones (I could see this on the photographs; one of them was from 1940, right before Stefanida's death, and it was as plain as day there, along with the magical hands of her husband, with his short, white fingers – on the photograph – that were on Stefanida's shoulders; Stefanida was seated). Jaglika thought, and people of her ilk always thought this way, that 'foreign medicines' were simply clever, including those foreigners arriving from various lands that the ship *Kumanovo* brought to Dubrovnik in 1936. Jaglika had a very good memory, and I've already said that one should not doubt the memory of a demiurge; she said that in August of '36 there were, just on that ship alone, a thousand of them, of the foreigners.

Jaglika also remembered January of 1940. She was in Zagreb, and there were unthinkably large crowds, waiting for the regent, Prince Paul; she said that everyone who was supposed to be there, was there, and that Croatian politician Maček himself delivered 'that famous welcome speech'.

What could she do, in January of 1940, at the train station in Zagreb, our Jaglika listening to those sublime words about his majesty, his wisdom regarding the two peoples, connected with the 'peace-loving Princess Olga?' What could she do then, or a little after that? She thrust deep into the pocket of the warm coat that she'd made from her own stock of cloth, the little Orthodox god of her father, and the big Catholic one of shiny brass – like the cross on the little chain around her neck – she brought out and held in her hands, when she clapped, like the other 100,000 souls present were doing there at the station; and again when she danced (with the brass in her hands) after Maček finished, in the name of the Croatian people, his welcome speech, wishing the Regent and his wife, Princess Olga, a 'pleasant stay'.

The year 1941 found her still in Zagreb. That was when her two relations vamoosed without a trace – at least as far as she'd tell us; she came back to Nikšić; in that grocery shop. There was nothing for the upcoming years of war; it was shuttered and sealed; naturally enough, and the other stores also went under. But Jaglika nonetheless wept only on account of the grocery shop in Nikšić. Of the people who burnt it down in the last year of the war, Jaglika never once said 'May God grant that not even their carcass should remain!' But Jaglika's mercantile mentality was, however, indestructible. She almost never spoke of the war years; she'd only mention, once in a while, on the subject of Stefanida's burial: 'Well, it was wartime, and war is what it is.'

XXI

I think that not even the late Stefanida, nor her probably also deceased Armenian husband, may God grant peace to both of their souls, could devise as effective a medicine against insomnia as what I came up with myself: first a plan came to mind that had sincere and courtly aims, and that meant: humiliation, penitence, obedience, and everything that appertains to those, to intensify them to the upper limit, but by no means beyond it: hard-heartedness, recalcitrance, nervousness (that's a little matter that people, uneducated people, think is physiological), decisiveness, conviction, and the rest, to drop to the lower limit, but by no means below it. The preparations take two or three hours, but in such a way that, for the last half an hour, you have to multiply to an infinite degree (if it's possible) the efforts to attain the feeling that you are an idiot; swill. And so, here's how I did it (this is, it's true, only one of the ways): I watched television till the channel went off the air, and beyond; the TV was on continuously, as was the radio; then in a rather synchronized fashion I turned on everything in the house (appliances and the rest of it) that was capable of tapping, banging, gurgling, singing, shrieking, burning, heating up, and so on, on down the line, the lights were switched on too, of course; then I would participate with all my heart in the whole uproar, more or less with confidence, if not totally artlessly. In the final fifteen minutes, I would have deceit kick in: 1) I repeat out loud: 'I do not want to sleep, what do I need sleep for, I'm going for a stroll'; 2) I get dressed, I put on my shoes, I place a cap on my head – without regard for the time of year or any other kind of time; I carry out all these actions (there's only one plot, because of the goal), patiently, attentively, and that means without that physiology, or more precisely, nervousness. After that, I walk outside; the walk is also a ruse: two laps, or two and a half, around the building, and then I come back with slow steps – this is premeditated: in the lift (even in the lift) I repeat loudly: 'I will take that book, and that one, too, plus a dictionary.' Furthermore: I sit down on the bed, with my shoes on, and the hat on my head (the bed is, of course, unmade), I take up only the dictionary and to myself, very seriously, I say out loud: 'pay attention to this, remember this ... ' After about half an hour I slept as soundly as a baby, or as soundly as a moribund (like Jaglika), with her shoes on, and a cap, on an unmade bed. It turned out well, quite well, like some sleight of hand for people who don't wear caps, but who should, constantly, summer and winter, or to be more exact, without regard for the time of year, or for time in general, as in Jaglika's day.

And Jaglika? Rolled up in her fifteen blankets, affixed to the rocking chair, with pom-poms on her slippers, the red ones, and with her glasses, always with her glasses on the tip of her nose, day, night, at noon – always; but even though, for a certain period of time, she hadn't seen anything – neither with them nor without them; most definitely, if Jaglika were really a good servant of God, she would grasp the idea that it was necessary to get rid of the glasses (back when, back then when she lost her sight), and not to put them away, on a shelf, or on the window sill, or under her pillow – I mean get rid of them, make them disappear – like a gangster in a good old thriller; because she would see again through the intervention of God's emissary, after she'd passed through the gates of death. To her misfortune, Jaglika had, however, more faith in technology and medicine, in the Pharisees that is, than in God and his emissaries.

I shouted in the voice of a thirty-year-old wretch, who neither does business nor thumbs her nose at God and God's will in anything at all, but rather, ruefully prays and suffers, and despite that barely clings to life, and who has not a trace of joy, nor at least a trace of balm; nothing; envious and enraged at Jaglika's ninety years, at Jaglika's sense of satisfaction in that rocking chair – opposite the window; at Jaglika's fortifying sleep, peaceful, after which she awakens ready for ninety more years. And I, with my puffy eyelids, legs, and hands, unready for another single day; I prayed (thinking of Jaglika's brass crucifix around her neck, and the other cross under her pillow) to disappear, not to die and not to live, but disappear like a gangster, and in a film with no sequel; with hatred, which concludes with a sentence uttered from the sidelines, out of the silence, like an ambush, slyly, however it had to be – when one is making common cause with mysterious forces (for help I even called upon the spirit of Stefanida and the spirit of her Armenian, for who knows all the things they know their way around in, the pair of them there in Istanbul, and they probably at least know enough about these things here to hang their hats on): let Jaglika die, and then me; may Jaglika die first, immediately, now, this minute... I'm watching already... let Jaglika die first, and Marina, and Danilo, one after the other, dear God please, precisely in this order, let them disappear. I prayed devotedly for their deaths. It didn't work; I was unable to say the prayer loudly, softly, or in a whisper – into my own ear and although not entirely to myself, rather convincingly.

XXII

It occurred to me, unexpectedly and abruptly, like when a pebble pings on a watery pane of glass, that my idiotic, passionate abandon (laziness?) could not go unpunished. If there were not, everywhere around me, an entire forest of diligent women, all kinds of diligent women, if they didn't have their malice and their severity, I would feel intimately connected to my own laziness, inseparably, and I would not sweep it away or exchange it for someone else's, not for anyone's, no matter whose, never, I'd manage not to do that, even if from now on into the future I needed to continuously wear a cap on my head, like on the shorn head of Marina Tsvetaeva. I say there is nothing of all that in the painful and tedious system of merits: merit at work, for the fatherland, for the family, for one's enterprise in general, and et cetera (I'm not mentioning that welter of others, the most painful ones: the medals or decorations, of the first order, the second, the third, the fourth, for instance), Jaglika with her merited retirement, the rocking chair and the window across from it; Marina with her well-deserved dead first husband, his merited retirement, and her meritoriously earned second husband; my merited boss, who is deservedly grateful to the mother of God (he put up a stone tablet to her in Zagreb, on that stone wall in Kamenita Street – in gratefulness for his health, his fifty years of life, a child, a wife, everything earned, for the glory and honour of the mother of God). And so, it is when your own mind fails you – a round pebble, shit stuck on a bird's wing, on a bench in the park across the street from the library, as happened to me. It's no longer possible (or maybe only temporarily so) to flee from fear, from the reddened, hysterical, worthy, multiplied faces of Jaglika, Marina, and the Boss – which are shrieking, suffocating me, screaming, even attacking animals, stirred up as if they were excited from head to toe, like postponed sexuality, or Catholic priests: he who eats bread cannot survive, and do not create him by the sweat of your brow and God's in a world that is bursting with creation, with work, according to God's will, for the glory of God, and to our joy and well-being, may the loaves of bread grow and swell women's stomachs, may they grow and shrink and so forth forever and ever amen.

I (or, more precisely: my body) neither swell up nor burst open, neither like bread – the zealous worker – the heavy labourer, nor like a woman's stomach, with the exception of when, at the beach, I'd glimpse some firm, real man's thighs, overgrown with light brown hair, and the balled-up package, that mythological package, underneath a pair of Speedos with the American flag on it. But maybe it didn't happen like that; maybe I never did, under any circumstances. And I kept on extending and then breaking off my sick leave, extending it and interrupting it; serious investigations of me (my body) were at issue; my boss was surely thinking (with delight?) that I wasn't going to survive! Or, what is more likely: my boss knew that there was no illness in my body anywhere, but he couldn't bet against there being one in my soul (my Achilles' Heel); he was keeping it to himself, however. I have no idea why my boss wasn't talking; maybe he had a good understanding of hypochondria! But really, if that's the case, then how did this miracle of good-natured patience manage to sneak into his big ugly head, into his colossal fatty body, into his squeaky voice, and cause all this, this uproar in him; as if I had secretly sent him someone who spoiled his fun, or the wrong key, or something along those lines, but the point is that my boss was confused, and his motivation (relating to heroic labour citations) dwindled. Or a tiny solution to an equally tiny enigma was concealed in my boss's doppelgänger. My boss had a double. His double came into the library exactly half an hour after the start of my workday. He'd roll in like this, this big gut through the narrow doors, inaudibly (the doppelgänger has rubber soles; all doubles have rubber souls, or none at all) and all at once overflowing with life and imagination it (the big gut) stands there dumbfounded before me. And what do I see, I simply don't believe it, I take off my glasses, I put them back on, take them off, put them on, rub my eyes – of course, oh hell, that's exactly it: a pink-white face like a child's rear end, the face of a forty-year-old is the butt of a five-year-old, this is uniquely stupid – smooth, without a shadow, or a wrinkle, with no possibility for you to hypothesize as to how you possibly encounter anything at all on that face other than a vast pink soft whiteness and watery eyes – there was nothing to differentiate the rest of it (there was nothing else there), for example, no mouth was in evidence, due to all the lard.

Consequently, my boss's double, a.k.a. the gluttonous mass of meat, massed from the neck down and from the neck up, impudently, persistently came and did what he usually does: swarms over me, with his weight, tries to force me to lay hands (as if I were asking for alms) on his stupid member, and softly pushes his face between my breasts, slimes me with his watery eyes, that's how he demanded everything of me, how the soft white creature made its demands…

And fine, a person, any person, might think even soft white creatures with arses instead of faces have the same needs, and stuff like that, as those others, un-soft and slightly prettier creatures…

There's no doubt that God arranged things this way. But none-theless it appears, nonetheless, it's not advisable to pile up, one alongside the other, like firewood – like chunks of human meat as well, divine affection for all the shapes that God created over and above the unfitness of the physiological (!) desires of my boss's white double for me.

I'm spouting nonsense; my boss's doppelgänger is an intelli-gent man (he writes successfully for television, as does my boss), despite having the arse of a five-year old child on his neck instead of his head – incidentally, my boss's double burst unexpectedly (!) into the library with a rather vague intellectual requirement – this was last summer: 'Which book should I take with me, on summer vacation?'

'Take a summer one.'

'What do you mean… a summer one?'

'OK, well, I mean a summer book, a book that can swim, sun-bathe, and the rest of it.'

'And you're… haha… that's like a… eh? Eh?' (The face – the child's arse – stretched into something resembling a smile, like chewing gum; let's say: on a popular television commercial.)

'I was being serious; there exist half-spring, summer, winter ones, one after the other, books, you understand, like all the rest of it.'

'Fine. Which book do I take?'

'Well, do you want something about animals, about bestiality too by the way?'

'I don't like animals.'

'Then do you want something about ontological and ordinary orgasms?'

'Who's the author of that one?'

'Plato, on the desires of creatures and the desires of the body. Haven't you read it?'

'I have. I read it.'

'Then why the question?'

'Lidia, do you want me to tell you something interesting?'

'I do not. Interesting is boring.'

'Listen, Lidia, I've watched people drink water from a tap without having a glass in their hand.'

'I'm not listening.'

'It's very interesting, Lidia … They all turned their heads to – '

'Write a television series, or the script for a commercial on how to drink water.'

'They did this with their heads – '

'Listen, it only seemed interesting to you. Anyway, this is just a bunch of hogwash that you're trying to force on me! Do you want a book or not?'

He left, after taking the smallest book possible: *The Memoirs of Capt. John Creighton*, the one in that cool red hardboard cover. What's he going to do with that? And from that day onwards, he began coming by regularly. At first I thought that he was my boss's twin brother, in the flesh, and later, that he was his regular brother; it turned out later, after a while, that the two of them have neither blood ties nor any other kind; I realized that it was a matter of just being the boss's double; in the beginning this unusual phenomenon entertained me; but later on complications emerged; the doppelgänger turned up whenever the boss was on the road; he never showed up when the boss was not away on a trip. My work at the library began to split in two. I had two bosses, the first one on the left side and the second on the right, like Jaglika had two gods. Boss number one, and boss number two; god the first and god the second – and everything was believable, as if that sequence or order did not exist, as if there were no rankings at all. So, yeah. I remained at home more and more; I took double sick leave, one for my boss, the other for his double; definitely, double seals and stamps, documents, and the rest; it required double the effort from me: two long mornings in the courtyard of the outpatient clinic, on a bench; at least that's how I managed to make the acquaintance of two little girls whose mothers were doing their sick leave with two doctors in the same clinic as mine. It's completely superfluous to describe them; and they wouldn't be able, even if they wanted, to reveal the secret of the tenderness that they constantly displayed for each other before my eyes.

A Story from Childhood

Oh, when was it; that event, like an unlikely theft, one under improbable circumstances in the middle of the day – logically – and therefore under the one thousand per cent vigilance of the residents of the entire city and its surroundings, to be sure, all the newspapers wrote (which demonstrates perfectly that they have nothing to write about); I was completely alone, in the large, very much colossal, confines of a hotel; nowadays, as far as I'm concerned, it could have been the premises of some terribly significant institution, like the Ministry of the Interior, for instance, or a foreign embassy, but it wasn't. It was a hotel. For a long while I was umming and ahing about what I should steal (in my childhood days I stole, incessantly almost, all over the place, without any obvious need): a jade ash tray, a little ceramic dish for ice cream, or a silver dinner plate with some additional wooden dishes, containing the remains of a red foodstuff. All at once, I decided on (it will never be clear to me what had such an unexpected influence on my choice) the medical supplies in a box meant for confectionery. I shoved it into my handbag and made for the door. The best thing would have been for me to open the door quickly and noiselessly and slip away; but at that moment someone rang the bell: the postman was at the door (hale and hearty) – and, but of course, everything was like in children's stories: the postman is righteous and he hates thievery with all his heart and soul, he's deeply tanned and dangerous – that is, strong; therefore I, probably, think right at that moment how that righteous giant of a man is going to separate my little head from my slender neck, and then, in lieu of that whole drama, he shoves a package under my nose and growls: 'Sign for it, little one!' I, apparently confused, refuse, wondering what in the … Maybe I also tell him that the little package wasn't for me, but he in the instant that followed relieved me of all doubts, growling once more though now with more of a bite: 'C'mon, don't dawdle. Sign it, girl!'

In the little package were scores of UNICEF greeting cards, the agreeable little designs with roosters and hen houses and the other little objects as well, but here was also a tiny metal badge with Peter Pan on it, and several pieces of paper with envelopes! The package was addressed to Marina. I don't recall exactly when I left that building, but, upon arriving home, I said not a word to anyone, nor did I display in any way any of the evidence of what had happened: Peter Pan, the greeting cards, and the medical supplies I shoved under the carpet – in that corner, that portion of rug that was under the cupboard in the living room. Later it was revealed, however, that I had not gone unobserved: the next day there was nothing under that carpet. Everybody was played dumb. I attempted several times – over the course of the following days – to start a story, sort of from far away, about how I'd had a few items, and how maybe some thieves had broken in, and did anything else go missing, other than my petty objects, but no one, a grand total of no one, had anything to say, a big fat nothing, as if I had cooked up the whole issue in a fit of delirium – which no one, truth be told, will ever know. Maybe.

XXIII

For ten days I tried unsuccessfully to reach Milena by telephone, and here's what was really happening: Milena disconnected her phone, and I know this for a fact now, in her intervals of dining, making out, ritual showering, sleeping, sleeping with L., sleeping without him; the remaining calls, which were an encouraging sign, whenever it would happen that the line was busy, and for a while right after… no one ever picked up – but they did show that Milena sometimes availed herself of the phone from time to time between these disconnections. I started dreaming of how I might ring her up; the telephone turned into Milena, and Milena became a telephone. Milena as the handset and its little holes that were dirty green in colour; and when, on day eleven, I managed to connect with her, it was as if I were holding, instead of the receiver, in my quivering, perspiring hand, Milena herself, live and in the flesh; upon hearing her voice, it immediately became clear to me that it's impossible to consort with a god when you yourself are not one!

But I should probably conceal, in an interior pocket like a thief, what it was that rolled so smoothly across my tongue, and palate, and teeth, that slippery non-existent sweaty sentence: 'I wish we could get together' – I said it calmly, it was drawn out, slimy, like when you pull money out of your pocket, with that same silly and unnecessary slowness. But I couldn't endure, right then, or actually at any time, the reaction of Milena's disgusted and slightly indifferent face to a different possible sentence: 'Milena, I must, must see you' – that would make no sense, after all, in a way identical to that first sentence.

Milena then, after a fairly short silence, said something about two or three topics, mentioned her L., yawned two or three times, and that was it. And now Milena, lowering the receiver, told L., just as she had told me, earlier: 'I'll have a cigarette after you're done with your snack.' What a tactic! So perfect, in every case, no matter what. I should ask her, for Danilo's sake, ask her to stick her moon-face in at Svetosavska at least for a minute. But I didn't. I did nothing of the sort. Danilo is convinced that I drove Milena away, and about envy he says truthful things: it starts from the middle of one's stomach then down, along an unknown axis, jagged and long. It was hard to explain to Danilo that L. loves Milena a lot more, I mean, in general and from whichever angle you look at it, L. loves Milena so much, much more, and more and more … incomparably more, even more than Danilo's redoubled hatred of me, and my small quantum of hatred and small quantum of love for Milena. Anyway, he never felt (saw) the shape and length of Milena's calves, and then the two dimples, the two dimples on the inside of her thighs, way up high, sensitive to everything in the world, like eyes; so it's just that much easier for him, or very much the opposite. I don't know for certain, but doesn't Danilo also have a big rock in his stomach, as do I, and the two of us, as relates to Milena, come across as two sides of the same coin.

In the library I frequently charge people fines, and I stuff the money in the left pocket of my coat, cool as a cucumber, and tear up the receipts. An unnecessary precaution! No patron would ever think to parade his or her receipt (the duplicate being in my possession) in front of my boss's nose, or his doppelgänger's, for the purpose of casting out a demon, 'coz what would that do for a reader's life; those are matters for bill collectors, wicket-workers, waiters, and maybe even the taxpayers. Every half hour I dash off to the bathroom; oh, what magic charms masturbation possesses! On the warm wall (because of the heating units in operation) my icy body, and across from me, well-thumbed books, arranged in stacks reaching to the ceiling. *The Confessions of Felix Krull, Confidence Man*, in a blue hard cover, and after that *Eugénie Grandet*, and so forth, and a few dictionaries; the upper part of my body leaning against the wall, because of my shoulders (as if someone else put them there) – actually, with the lower part of my body inclined away from the wall, and improbably accustomed to my fingers. I have lived so long without Milena; now I place her moon-head where it belongs. Afterwards I turn the tap on, wash my hands – psychological and quasi-psychological interpretations are pointless; the washing of one's hands is not a gimmick done with the super-ego, and with your ancient forebear, who is forever wagging a threatening finger, nothing to do with that bullshit parade of words from the so-called archetypal homelands, but rather, quite simply: on my fingers, my thumb, my index and middle fingers, remain the recognizable scent of Milena's pussy, definitely not mine; all that grunt work has little do to with me; Vespasian accurately calls it momentary illusion, and naturalness, although it would look like something else to my boss, and to his double too.

XXIV

The month of May is not exactly the greatest time to die, or especially to be buried; Jaglika spent the whole night dying, horribly slowly. Danilo was sitting in his room; he would show up periodically and ask, and keep on asking: 'Is that her soul, Lida, those little white bubbles?' Or: 'Surely that's the soul, right, Lida? What else could there be that's white like that? Give her some water. Can't you see she's thirsty, Lida!' He came back every half hour to look: 'Not yet. Those little bubbles are still coming out.' And he looked amazed. He seemed to be off his rocker. *Daaaaaammit!* Jaglika and I passed the entire night, in fact, alone. I should've left her in peace.

At first she was just a little yellow, and later she was yellow all over; and by morning she was dead; she was with God, completely white and totally pure. For days before that she'd been repeating: 'I never did anything nasty to anybody.' And Danilo tried to cheer her up: '*Baba*, stop it with those stories about sin. How did that one curse go in Hungarian; come on, granny, that curse in Hungarian? Fuck you and your copper angel whistling on seven weeping willows, granny, was it whistling or playing the flute? Eh, *Baba*? ... ' But Jaglika, who had long since forgotten the language of her mother, would say: 'Not seven but ten, d'you understand Danilo, ten willows.' And Danilo bustling around the rocking chair holding the half-dead Jaglika, stubbornly: 'Come on, *Baba*, in Hungarian, please Granny ... ' Jaglika wasn't paying attention to the fact that everybody was asking her, the real angels and the souls of the dead, to speak Hungarian, and then to think back and tell us about things from the time when she had two or three shops; it couldn't be worthwhile; even I wouldn't be worth it, not to mention Danilo's wish to hear just one curse in her mother's language, in her language. Jaglika counted off her sins on the fingers of both her clenched hands, as if she were totting up the receipts from the last two hours at her shop in Nikšić; or as if she were stacking groceries on the shelf opposite the door in that same store in Nikšić.

In the morning, when she was dead, she had the face of an embryo; everything was erased, by the hand of a copper angel and by the hand of the Jesus on the wall. The coroner, that graveyard doctor, arrived, pulling on a pair of transparent plastic gloves. He turned the stiff, deceased (having now been introduced to this god and that one), and now angelic Jaglika first onto one side of her body and then the other – like a small, planed tree trunk; he unbuttoned her shirt, felt for her pulse through her breast, and then flipped her over on her back and tapped two or three times with his fingers. Danilo said over and over from the doorway: 'Be careful, be careful, she'll break, I mean it for God's sake watch out!' Then the coroner sprinted off to the bathroom, tripping over his own feet, washed his hands, threw the plastic bag-gloves onto the floor, pressed a piece of paper with an official stamp on it into Danilo's hand (saying that Jaglika died a natural and not a violent death), and left, taking two steps at a time on his way down. Before his visit I had washed Jaglika, and dressed her; Čeda of Little River helped me – he had come half an hour after getting Danilo's phone call. He was panting, and growling: 'My God, is she heavy!' Danilo lugged the washbowls in and out, muttering fretfully every time: 'Is there really more, Lida? What is this?' Meanwhile the vital fluids just poured out of Jaglika, and after they placed her in the coffin, they kept on; puddles remained on the bed.

All Marina did was send a telegram, and send money, by wire; so that her mother would be buried where she wanted, but she said she wouldn't be able to come to the funeral, because all the transport workers in the world were on strike; bull-shitter. But none of us knew where it was that her mother wished to be buried: here, there, *waaaaaaay* over *heeeere*. Then Čeda suggested that I give him the money for everything, and he would take care of it all hunky-dory. So Jaglika was cremated; there was no room for her under the earth here, and no room there, but only in the oven. The most random set of relatives flooded into the house, blew through in perilous bursts, and one after another they grew irate and started talking all this bullshit about Christianity, 'a decent burial', 'just not like this, burning her up', and all the rest of it.

XXV

Vespasian's letter: Dear Lidia, what I'm sending you now is my tuppence worth on the idiocies connected with the so-called 'woman question'. My text consists of two sections, as you'll readily see; the first is a pretend pamphlet – yeah, right! But the second part is a description of my own experience when I was still mobile and could still serve (that, you know, is the swindle about usefulness to society, the dogmatic hocus-pocus: We are all building this together, we stand ready… and so forth, and you know, yourself, why). I've already mailed it to the editors of a daily newspaper, but they rejected it. One observation, Lidia: first: I hope that you aren't so dumb as to think that my general (interior and external) dissatisfaction with my wife is the reason for my writing all of this; you're familiar with that unhappiness from my earlier letters; second: I also hope, or better, I expect you not to react the same way as the aforementioned person. When I showed her the finished text, all she did was brush it off, make a squeamish expression, and say: 'Phooey. I thought that you were at least literate, at least in terms of mechanics, even if you don't have any brains.' In the event that this should occur to you, I will find out about it somehow. Consider this first: you belong to that enormous majority of unintelligent women, and you are by no means, not one little bit, any different from the horde of insatiability and stupidity that is regrettably throttling our civilization. And secondly: consider this letter of mine the last in my series of attempts to converse only from one side, in accordance with my codices, for you are a woman, and all women are curious and talkative (always, always, always) and I am consequently certain that you've greedily devoured all my letters, read each one of them multiple times even, and that you'll read this one all the way through. I know that, little Lidia; you do not possess enough indifference to chuck this letter, just as you haven't tossed out any of them before when they were unread. Now, on to those two texts, or whatever you wish to call them, but Lidia, do not fail to take these warnings seriously, I beg of you. The first text is also in the form of a letter (I sent it to the newspaper), and letters are, you know, appealing because of the direct contact – from only one side; there can be no answer, right, Lidia!

'My dear working and non-working women, it wouldn't be a bad thing if, for once, you were to inquire about whether or not your stretched-out pelvises could be used to make seals and stamps for use in government offices, and ultimately for any kind of offices in general, seals and stamps for various and sundry files on which depends the fate of the world; otherwise known as metallic orders and decorations for success and merit. Does anyone at all benefit from your inflated and fabricated tenderness? I know that you all know, right down the line (no matter how dumb you pretend to be) that civilization had to develop, *inter alia*, as a colossal effort to rein in (and sometimes destroy) your collective sexual insatiability, your potency, which is in essence, seeing how it's unlimited, destructive. In this thousand-year labour, the male sex has lost all its power, its biological power, and now it is faced with its own annihilation. Your irrationality has resulted in rationality. Fortunately for everyone around the world, you all lack the wisdom to know how to deal with this fact. Some among you whine about women's issues, or the woman question, or whatever that marvel is called, while others among you bray hysterically about feminism, and all of you live in the shared error that your fat or skinny, small or large arses, your powdered faces, your grievous sexual troubles, the hair on your legs – that these are more important than the emblem or trademark of an export-import firm. But this is how things look: whenever some of you, or maybe even all of you, come home from work, scream at your husband or your children that there's no lunch to be had, your husband scarpers out the door, he doesn't give a fuck about feminism or what you're shouting, and then his mother, with whom you're living gives you this rot about how for example her son could find someone who's if not better than you at least more hard-working and calm. In the evening your lawfully wedded one mounts you with his full imagination, while you lack imagination, your right arm goes to sleep and his big and always damp stomach nauseates you, but you console yourself with the fact that that stomach is at least legitimate, and that little bit of woe, down below, is legit too. You even get insomnia, oh, the horror, that weak-willed soft man, that lukewarm boring world. And while sleeplessness has you in its grips you remember, you think back all of a sudden, to your mother's words about marriage, the sacred institution of marriage, about how for instance they're all the same, et cetera, and embracing that lukewarm wet stomach you fall asleep in the blink of an eye like a baby.

The family hearth, your mother would have said, is the strongest flame in the world. Later on you or some of you, or indeed all of you, succeed in snatching a lover, who like the rest is non-committal, old, boring, and dumb, but its status is all right, and its legitimacy. And never and I mean never would you be able to do better; your imagination is wanting, my dear ladies, you're never going to have it, and that's why life and the world are so difficult for you. This whole lousy brouhaha about feminism comes down to this: it bothers every one of you, whether you're big-arsed or small-arsed, it's all the same all over the world, every one of you, lame, mute, deaf, hysterical, schizoid, whatever, you forget them when necessary: you would give up everything, status, parties, factions, and the rest of it, for one single hand, a moist masculine one. If only you knew how to effect this sickly sweet and vulgar substitution: the state for the little wet hand of a man. Therefore, be intelligent, the way you've been since time immemorial. Think with passion about your elastic vaginas and uteruses, stretchable enough for you to envelop the world several times over; what more do you need? And the imagination, which you do not have, leave it out of the picture, since anyway it has no connection, and you all know this quite well, to the mechanics and the superficiality of your own big ugly bodies, your patches of unwanted hair, powders, cosmetics, ultimately, your being!

And now this little social game, in this country, in this city, in these times: at the opening of an exhibition of a famous painter, in an equally famous gallery, a large number of people had gathered: the usual suspects: so-called intellectuals. They giggle with one another, turn on each other, flirt around, etc. Later a small group split off, and I was among them; we went to a nearby café: The Twenty-five Lotuses. We sat down at a rectangular table in this order: the female editor of a Zagreb newspaper, with perky hair and face and breasts to match, a theatre and film critic for a Belgrade paper; a guy whose hair was black and shaggy and who everybody thought for some ungodly reason was a cop; a tall blonde woman, she was, I assume, someone's wife, or lover; that's six of one, half a dozen of another; the point is that she looked like the perfect orgy

machine, and in addition to that, which was not without significance, she also worked in the newspaper business – for the culture
section. *Ach ja*, I almost forgot the actor; he was a renowned stage
actor from Zagreb; and around him was a multitude of chicks – oh,
for fuck's sake, no, there wasn't a single one; that night he would
remain confoundedly alone. They all scattered: the interesting ones,
the blondes, brunettes, the ones with tits, the ones with arses, with
stocky legs and slender legs, and the ones with their cute little eyes,
oh definitely, back at the exhibition. I don't think anyone was as
abundantly repulsed by the whole superficiality and emptiness of
the exhibition, or of the high-rolling city types, the café, the tomcats – or whatever else you call that breed of man – as I was? But
let's leave sentiments out of this for the moment, even if they are
appropriate, as mine are. For a moment the orgy machine looked
like a dragon; everyone was quivering behind the table, seeing the
way she devoured one roasted red pepper after another, right down
to the stem; later he shoved my supper under her nose, too, with
the gratitude of a good cow – big, flaring nostrils (they moved
rhythmically), and she wolfed it down, in no more than three bites;
meanwhile people were conversing about chess, domestic literature,
this poet and that poet, Greek libraries, Greek statues, sculptors ...
I left to go and vomit; then again; the orgy machine dined, if I'm
not mistaken, three times, and I threw up three times, or even
four, and I had an empty stomach, by way of contrast to hers,
etc ... The rest of the spectacle isn't important, nor was the one
before it; none of these parades are ... To sum up: thanks to the
various orgy machines of the female sex, that impotent minority,
I believe, that is the male world forces on the remaining majority
of the female world – whose orgasms are guided by imagination –
the bullshit about their frigidity, supporting and applauding all

the orgy machines (which are to be found only among persons of the female sex; persons of the male sex, impotent, half-potent, thoroughly satisfactorily potent, always have imagination). So now, my dears, imagine the fabulous connection, the civilizational link: between the trembling simple mass of women and impotent men – whom the most perfect prostheses would not help; but as I said already their weakness passes thanks to their imagination; the female orgy machine is a unique kind of *perpetuum mobile.* So there's no confusion, so you won't proclaim me to be the one who speaks rashly about issues that are, obviously how many thousands of years old, thank you very much … not taking into account other things in connection with the first, a third thing in connection with the second, and once more the first thing in connection with the third; and if you please, the one who does all of this from a sense of leisure of an afternoon stuffed with momentary and in all like-lihood groundless embitterment, in the fatuous use of skin on the fingers of the left and right hand (from yellow fire ants one should make crumbs, transform their otherwise living crushable crumbi-ness devoutly into actual dead little crumbs, little brownish dots. I mean, and instead of into an ashtray, after a sufficient number of them have been assembled, pour them imperceptibly into the bun of hair on your wife's head; although this appears, this only appears to be the cleverer variant: to pack them away in big bags together with the winter clothes and some lavender), therefore, in order that no confusion might arise, I offer myself up generously for all possible future discussions on a similar theme, if not an identical one, without corporeal favours, if you don't mind, in that sense I'm pretty much useless, and besides, we need to draw a strict line between theoretical matters and non-theoretical ones. I have about all of this many more thoughts on first, second, and third issues;

this should be obvious, thank you very much: on many issues, and not just the ones I've written down. It wouldn't be clever to exclude me or, well, consider my contribution to be antlike, that is to say, crumb-y – hopelessly small, and ridiculous, as the case may be. We're talking about naiveté; one should not confuse that with good will or hard work. To the extent that everything is together, in the entire run of things both first and second, and third and sundry, it cannot seem like much if the entire future image is the image, actually, of meaningless yellow ants, and then we should not disregard the fact that yellow ants, small and accustomed to extermination (which is the proper relation to have to one's fate, not taking it too seriously), are nonetheless persistent and enduring. Nonetheless, dear working and non-working women, that would be a strategic move on the level of a tragedy from ancient times!'

I had a good laugh, and then I was quiet for a similar length of time, and I came across to that guy in the window as a very serious person, and at the end of this parade, as is the case with Vespasian's wife, and for heaven's sake I am so much like her in so many ways, I said out loud: 'Fie, fie, fie' – there was a threefold similarity to her, and it was solidarity, for Pete's sake. I swiftly signed the letter, both parts of it (that first part addressed to me as an intro, and the second one, which they did not print in the newspapers) and crammed it into the drawer. I don't know – I would not dare confirm or deny (in the hour of judgement, the difference is effaced), whether I suspect something or do I not, but after this letter that is, I must admit, rather hysterical, nothing else came, ever, not one single letter, and not just not from Vespasian. Through some infernal channel, had Vespasian managed to find out about those three sequential utterances of 'Fie'; or did he simply assume in advance that I would say them, those three words, three times, loud and clear? Or did he devise the whole thing as a deceit? Maybe Vespasian disappeared, flew the coop, died, met Jaglika – but how would he recognize her? And so, he's just gone away – under the earth or to another country, which comes out to be the same thing. However it happened, and whatever happened with him, Vespasian has earned on account of exaggerated hysteria his bit of scorn, like a little yellow ant, squished between your thumb and forefinger; due to his malice, too, and the rest of what he did not show but was visible; such figures, although they are made of paper, should be pushed aside with one hand then the other, and very loudly, but without any cursing or spitting (that is so unnecessary), one should say: Fie. And then … start in on other figures, even if on paper, to the last: Fie.

XXVI

'Then he sat down in the boat, betrayed his friends, his fatherland, and his brothers … It's permissible, sometimes, to submit ingratiatingly to the powerful ones and deceive one's friends because of them – but only at a moment when we know clearly and reliably that it's the only way humanity can be saved. Up to this moment in time, Noah has been the only person to face this dilemma.'

(L.K. N.K.)

And just as things already following some mysterious orbit, like a path between the moon and that which is in its unyielding power, to which I succumb every time, over the years ever more similar to the first occurrence – in this way measurements of abridgement are foreshortened, and they slowly disappear. One person whom I trusted was Danilo's doctor. Doctor Kovač. How would Vespasian put it: a famous personality of this city, this era, this country; in connection with dumb things like this, and plenty more, the help of any and all miracle workers might come in handy, like Stefanida and the Armenian; using an alchemist's skill to transform everything, and what is left over from it all, into a pile of matter as inconsequential as dust – devoid of any value whatsoever, so that the whole affair is not, however, the calling down of the last judgement, or some similar era, and of the features associated with it, the devil is merrier in the Armenian's hands, in Stefanida's eyes, whoever needs more than that, let him or her seek it from God, the left-hand one or the one on the right! With Dr Kovač I was not making an exception of any kind; it was like that with other people, too; however, now, even to me, that selection appears rigged: Dr Kovač, and that means he's a psychiatrist, is Danilo's doctor; that very combination of words shows that I should have avoided this; but haven't I already said that these are the paths between sleepwalkers and the moon, and they're nothing but incomprehensible to others? And incidentally I have been, for a long time, since I've been aware of myself, outside of myself, outside of my own power – if that's to be understood as rationality, or something very similar to it. I told him all there was to say about myself, going from the end towards the beginning, bogging down around the mid-point; everything that was inside (but that 'inside' is, with me, not sealed, as it is with other people) I tossed out: I slopped – like a bucket of spit, rancid and stinky – all of it straight into Dr Kovač's face. More than anything else, Dr Kovač is a man firmly pinioned somewhere into his profession, with nails of iron: and he merely wiped off his face, politely, and he even smiled. He could not understand. He lacked the imagination – as Vespasian said, and therefore he was not capable of fathoming that the non-existence of power over himself (precisely because of that unusual distance and ambiguity) entails the existence of power over others. I was outside myself, but Dr Kovač was in my hand, later even more so. In this way I would spare anybody, in this case Dr Kovač, of the labour of deciphering my personality – I tipped it out unsparingly, together with the seeds, like a big busted watermelon, and simultaneously I was depriving him of the possibility of interpreting it. It seems like there is cunning in this, a pre-formulated guile, like you find among tomcats great and small, the phosphorescent slyness of a desperate individual. If a desperate individual (in this case, me) doesn't conceal his or her desperation, but on the contrary disseminates it across the entire field of vision, and the experience of others, then desperation blends into pure profit: other people are roped in with their parochial, closed, sealed souls, carefully tucked away like the wallets in their pockets. Therefore, setting people up, lying, tiny acts of devilment, everything in the name of desperation, results in a constant distancing from their own desperation and also their fear, and it goes so far as to resemble a form of freedom. After my unsuccessful fuck with Dr Kovač, not just because of the missing orgasms on his side and mine, but also because of the racking ordeal of the whole event; apropos of that, he had two or three almost painful ejaculations, but not a single orgasm; I started talking (and that wasn't bad, and it could even be considered rather good, when spitting outwards towards another face, onto another face, begins with nausea, even if it's physical). First of all, I recited a dream, which was, with a few changes, with little digressions from the real dream, submitted to him, like a picture, and thus: I was dreaming of Milena's mum; she was wearing some horrid light-coloured dress; she was bringing in children's shoes, and said: 'From Italy,' and she continued: 'Somebody should try them on, for heaven's sake; it wouldn't be right for me to have purchased them for nought.' Later on, it's unclear what became of those shoes. We went into the flat, on Svetosavska Street; a bunch of people turned up: Marina's husband, *inter alia*; Danilo leaning on a large pole. I curse (but without anger) at his mother, father, grandma, and at Mira, one after the other. We go into Jaglika's room, and someone is whispering in alarm, well nigh hysterically – and it turns into a shriek, how he or she has to get up early the following day because of some important errands, and that everyone, at that very moment, without any unnecessary delays, must lie down and go to sleep. But damn it, all the beds disappeared as if by a magic trick; in the next moment, which was unconnected to the previous goings-on, Danilo is taking a piss next to my head, and then he laughs, and a moment later he tries to have sex with me, thrusting himself on me in a way completely identical to how it was done by my boss's doppelgänger, my boss. Then, a few scenes from the beginning get repeated, the same way it works in a film; like in a montage, for example; more or less. Dr Kovač demands that I continue the story and he wants additional information: who is Milena, who's this, and who's that. And then he utters, with a smile, an obscurity: 'Those, Lidia, are your symbols, and only when you tell me more stuff will I be able to...'

Ah, how attentively that bald, heavyset psychiatrist with the loose blond hair listened to the following: in the evenings I am not able to close my eyes, for I am 100 per cent convinced that I will die if I do so, and when, finally, I do close them, after tremendous effort, then I am not able to open them; I will catch sight of myself there on the chair, across the room, on the floor, on the ceiling, several selves, large and elongated, and with her there, smiling at me, making fun of me, and then the guy on my bed whispers something to me... and so I die a number of times in the course of the night, and what should I do, what in God's name should I do, I ask Dr Kovač, the man who's famous in this city, and who people claim is famous in all the other cities. Danilo's psychiatrist asks: 'And you, Lidia, do you take drugs? Speak freely. We're friends, aren't we?' His hand lightly touched my knees; from the moment my stretchable vagina (they're all like that) swallowed his pink worm, the way the sea swallows an unskilled swimmer, forever and irreversibly, he was getting things confused, and I could even suppose that that wasn't unusual. At one time Danilo had been treated for excessive drug use, by this moronic nut-job from the Military Medical Academy, who later published these fascistoid articles about drug addicts, condensing in this way his medical experiment and his hatred, both reserved for the weak, eliciting the glittering support and solidarity of the strong. Therefore Dr Kovač mixed up a few things, not intentionally, it's true, but owing to an inadequacy of imagination; this shortcoming of his can picture hallucinations existing only in the realm of hallucinogenic drugs, if not in the sphere of outright insanity, and assorted other variants live outside his scope, permanently and definitely. The distance is indispensable, and so I swept away his bloated, damp hand from my knee, which was still there and bare, and said to him, 'Now, now. Please. You don't have to read Castaneda to grasp that Eastern societies and drugs have nothing in common with Western societies and the Freudian problems of our childhoods, our later impossibilities, and bad communication, and I think all this has been harmful to you. Somewhere along the line, you got all mixed up.' Castaneda's book lay open and face down on his desk, and a little farther over, standing stolidly on its plaster pedestal, was the plaster figurine of Freud. In order to get beyond himself, I advised him to experience it, the sooner the better (beyond literature) – it will be just as fine for him as it is for his little cock in my big pussy; drugs are not required, and even less so the mystical and phony connections of East and West, and least of all – or not at all necessary – is a move to the East, because it remains for all time separate: the Eastern world has its Eastern shifts and escapes, and the West has the rest and sometimes escapes, too, the Eastern way. But after it was all over, while I was pulling on my underwear, my spread legs were right next to the Castaneda and then directly (that blessed symmetry: West-East – and finally Danilo's doctor understood) above the head of the plaster statuette of Freud (this all took place in his office on the fourth floor). I say: 'And anyway this was all a load of shit, and unpleasant, and therefore unnecessary. I can't talk with a man who hasn't experienced any of this; the rationality of your science is as impotent here as a lamb before a slaughter; if you haven't ever felt that, then you don't have a chance, or better, you don't have an imagination; if you had just a stub or butt-end of talent it might still work; I mean, I could leave here at least with the illusion that it was worth it, fucking and talking to fill up the hour.'

But Dr Kovač, understanding everything at that moment: 'Stop. Don't go. I was thinking of prescribing you something, something mild, but now it's obvious to me what's going on… wait… ' I left, as is required, with a civil: 'Goodbye, Mr Kovač. You should forget the Castaneda, though… It won't mean anything to you… Goodbye.'

Dr Kovač told Danilo that he had slept with me, and that way the doctor won him over to his cause. I didn't doubt his medical intentions; obviously, he had to try somehow to wrest Danilo from my embrace, since he had fallen, headlong and hopelessly, into my arms after Milena and Jaglika left us, and he had entangled himself, embroiled himself with the chances of his ever being able to extricate himself growing ever slimmer as time passed. It was indispensable, it was, I swear by everything that's holy, hideously massively necessary for Danilo to start hating me and for my one-hour therapy session with his doctor to be a welcome thing for him, and for Dr Kovač too, but not for me. When we look a little more closely, two opposing and mutually exclusive feelings in Danilo's heart and soul could have resulted in either resolution or complete and definitive confusion. I believe that, all things considered, Danilo had very little chance, or no chance at all, in Kovač's disgusting racket! I would have loved to see Kovač take his esteemed right hand and castrate himself, voluntarily, with an expression of bliss on his face (bliss that is the result of recognition that one is once and for all being emancipated from the problematic needs of the body, of one part of the body if not all of it, and also, comprehending that other denouements are possible, not just those involving semen), and later he could give his member away as a Western relic, to some famous Western scholar, and they would rejoice in his sacrifice, never quite grasping that he had defrauded them in this matter, falsifying his false wish as a victim and thus wringing out of them yet another kind of admiration, by deceit. All the patients of both sexes, in their sessions of so-called group therapy or work therapy, would draw the face of the saintly psychiatrist, and they'd write his initial all over the place: K. And they'd knit that same countenance, and make little wooden carvings of it.

Instead, however, of these artless daydreams of mine, and what were ultimately my burning desires, it was all even more horrible: Danilo walked into my room and began to shout: 'You whore! You're just a whore who wants to climb into the sack with somebody all you want to do is fuck you're a whore just like Marina! Here's one goddam whore right here...' He took off his trousers and underwear and dropped them onto the floor and then burst out sobbing like a child. Danilo, the child of Marina. I tried to get stern, the way that all people are stern in this world towards rotten hysterical children, although in that moment my only sincere wish was to hug him and to cry, just like he wanted too. I shouted, nonetheless, hysterically: 'Get lost, you loser, get lost, get lost when I say so, you animal!' And Danilo, through his inconsolable and unstoppable wailing, a stream of tears, like an abused child: 'And Marina...Marina's just like you...You snatched everybody away from me; you two get under everyone's skin, and you drove Milena away, and everybody else, everybody...'

XXVII

Šopika and A. Caršov (The Friday Circle)

A wacked-out meeting; I made it there thanks to Little River Čeda, who for days and days after Jaglika's transition, probably to – the heavenly kingdom, continued to hang around our house. Good heavens, the kinds of people he knows! These guys, none of whom I have slept with, since they are an unattractive lot, right down the line, used to get together on Fridays. Typically, people would go to the apartment of one of them, who lived with his tomcat, and that would be the only living company he had in the course of the week (from Friday to Friday). There was no coffee, alcohol, hash, food, or anything else of that sort – just their discussions about the essence of life and God's participation in it. More precisely, the degree to which God was involved in it. But also about the parapsychological revolution, the principle of irrationality – which has to be established, rationally, on the back of several other propositions, and then everything would be mimeographed and passed around amongst ourselves, or to people outside the Circle only if they had three people to vouch for them. Everything had to stay horribly secret. Sometimes the more serious reports had to be skipped on account of sleepiness, general sleepiness, and the lack of ideas that arose from that. One guy, whose name I have forgotten, but who, I remember because he never took the hat off his head, it looked similar to a baseball cap, but without the brim in the front, and who always took off his shoes immediately upon arrival, wearing trousers and a jacket but barefoot; he always said the same thing (this was already the third Friday of this): 'Šopika (Schopenhauer) was as you know a pure genius, and Šopika as you know fucked Marx up, too, but so that we can see what kind of action we should take, whatever it might be, as you know I'm for doing it immediately, so how about everybody raises their hands, who's for it immediately, with no delay, and who's for later, so that it's all on the table, as you know I told you about that letter that I received from a certain Caršov from London, we have to check out whether he might be able to serve our cause even though as you will see he's a traditionalist; it all revolves around Christ, but here you go, I told you I was going to duplicate the letter for all members of our circle, and we should read it through, so that we can clarify right away whether to include Caršov in the movement or not, and so we know, on this question, who's for it immediately, with no postpone-ment, they should raise their hands and then, whoever isn't for it, whoever's for finding out, later.' At that point the guy distributed the letter to everyone. The letters on it were barely legible; he told me to forget that I was a woman and to stop tarting myself up, and that was making things harder, and he told me how I should know that in the movement no one had a sex, the revolution with its starting point as the principle of irrationality must have only comrades in its ranks, emancipated from their sexuality, and if anything along those lines should occur, it has to be checked out, investigated, to see whether it occurred on a human basis, friend-to-friend, and he kept on and added that if that conception of the world was not to my liking, then I could leave at once. One of the members had gone on his own into the adjoining room – to the place where the cat was; he was rocking back and forth on a chair and hummed: 'My mare *Suziiii*, Suzi *myyyy* mare' in long, drawn-out words.

The guy with the cap was the boss of everything, because when he ordered the dude on the chairs to stop singing and immerse himself in the material, the guy quit instantly. And this is how the letter looked: it was written on pieces of paper pulled out of a Bible, in Cyrillic:

'Dear Friend!

I am sending you herewith the final chapters of the Gospel of Luke. This is the second part, and we hope that you received the first part. If you didn't get it, we ask that you write to the following address:

Andrei Cartov (Caršov) B.C.M.

Box 4930

London W.C. IV (6 xx)

England'

'The Gospel of Luke is named after its author. Luke was a doctor and his report on Christ's life and his spiritual service is a lesson in sensitivity and practical applicability. He surveys for us Christ's love and care for people with broken hearts, for those who are ill and those who are grieving. Here, also, we have a description of Jesus Christ's trial and His crucifixion, and His ultimate resurrection from the dead and his appearances to the people who loved him.' This was written in Caršov's own hand; to it were appended several small sheets of paper photocopied from the Bible, with a few errors, which weren't all that major: the following chapters from Luke were there, from twelve to twenty-four, plus a small section from the start of the Gospel of John, Chapter One, but only these verses: fifty-one, fifty-two, fifty-three. Between chapters twelve and fourteen, in a small blank space on the printed page, Caršov wrote the following: 'Luke wants you and me, as the readers, to experience Jesus in a vital, personal way, because Jesus' love is revealed to us so clearly through his life and death. I implore God to give you spiritual understanding while you read, and to help you, dear friend, make the personal decision to invite the living Jesus Christ to be your saviour.'

At the end, after the fifty-third verse of John: 'And they were in the church constantly, praising and thanking God. Amen.' And to this whole packet of twenty-plus pages, Caršov had also added this: 'If all we do is agree, intellectually, with his teachings, then we will not grasp at all the purpose of his death. He requires of us that we make the decision to submit our lives to his authority. I would be overjoyed to hear back from you regarding your decision in this matter. Or perhaps you have some friend there who might partake in it with you. God has blessed you as you've been considering these things. I invite you to tune in to our radio show, which would bring you comfort.

Your devoted,
A. Cartov.'

That guy who'd been singing the song about his mare, Suzi, said he found all this to be boring and old hat and that the guy in Britain was a whinger, and anyway he didn't see any connection between the letter and the pages torn out of the Bible, which we all have, and our cause. The main guy, the chap with the hat, rebuked him, saying he hadn't grasped any of it, and that the whole trick, the whole deal, was concealed at the beginning, in those three x's, in the address, and that everything was just symbolic. Then he said: 'Raise your hands if you're for doing this right away, without delay, having Caršov join us, those who aren't for that, who are for it later, for Caršov being added in later, so we know.'

XXVIII

I only went to the Friday circle one more time; I had the firm intention of joining it like A. Caršov, without any skills of my own, but they threw me out for being unsuitable for membership, as they did to Čeda Little River, with the explanation that our moral qualities were atrophied and that the organization, that is, the movement, or rather, the future cosmic revolution, could not rely on us, not even at the outset.

Since Danilo had been walking around the house like a ghost for days and days on end (there's no way to count, to measure, time, that time), Kovač advised me by telephone to bring him, for him to go, to that place on Palmotićeva.

On the third floor, there is a nurse he'd fallen in love with; on the second floor, two of them; he says that he dreams of Dr Kovač. But on this subject, Kovač says: 'You know, Lidia, it's unclear what's nightmarish here: sleep, Danilo himself, Danilo's vision of me, or all of it together.' At that moment the phone rang in his room and Dr Kovač changed his stripes like a chameleon: he was conversing with the director and was fascinatingly condescending, just as he was fascinatingly amusing, that is to say, flirtatious, when he conversed with the nurses in the ward. Damn it, bombs are the most effective when they begin to drop, when they're whistling along, and that guy in the cap is right, it should happen immediately, without hesitation, who's for it, raise your hands!

A Thursday, July, the first Thursday, a visit to Palmotićeva Street: I brought Danilo clean laundry, apples, and cigarettes. Danilo inquired about Milena, and then about Milena again and Marina. 'How are you … I mean, you?'

'I'm fine, Danilo.'

'Are you sure you're fine?'

'Yes, Danilo, for crying out loud.'

'And how is my family?'

'What in the world do you mean by that, Danilo?'

"Well, my… Mum. Did Mum write, how is her health? You know, I worry about that, Lidia.'

'Listen, Danilo. Enough with the screwing around.'

'Why are you angry now, Lidia?'

'Mira sends her regards.'

'Does that mean that I don't need to be worried about Marina's health?'

'That's enough, Danilo, for God's sake. You know, I don't have to come here…'

'Wait, Lidia –' (Danilo grabbed me by the hand, brought his face close to mine, I could smell the odour from his mouth, Marina's odour [the two of them, I mean, their mouths, always had the same smell], clasped my fingers and mumbled:) 'Wait, but Milena why didn't Milena get in touch … and Milena what have you done to her what did you say to her what did you tell her Lida?'

'She, she called yesterday, and she told me to say hello to you …'

'Are you certain that she asked you to say hello and what else did she say?'

'She's going to come see you and she sends you a big hello.'

'Are you sure, Lidia?!'

'I'm sure, Danilo.'

On the second Tuesday in July, Dr Kovač was on call. I went into his office on the third floor. Dr Kovač said: 'Danilo is almost well, completely well; just a bit longer and we're going to release him. He's sleeping and eating well, and he isn't fighting with the other members of the group. Plus, he isn't refusing to cooperate, as he did earlier.' Then he mumbled something about how Danilo's depression was minor and how this wasn't 'all that awful'. 'Come back,' he said, 'next Thursday. I'm going out of town starting on Monday, but my colleague is standing in for me and you know him.'

The therapy sessions that Dr Kovač mentioned went like this – Danilo had talked to me about them earlier, and I also attended one myself: Dr X says: 'This is group therapy. The order of the day here is democracy and self-management. The point isn't just that everyone can speak up, but rather that everyone has to. Come on now, let's see who's going to be first.' Then one of the bleached-blonde nurses stands up (only nurses and sales clerks in the Centroprom grocery stores go blonde by using *Oksižen*, that is, pure hydrogen. *En masse*: in one spot there'll always be a dozen white-haired women with black eyebrows) and repeats the question. Then Psychiatrist X stands up and repeats the question, and for example one of these three persons named X says, for instance: 'So, Danilo, how were your dreams last night?' Danilo said of Dr X that he was as stupid as an asshole from the inside.

On the third Thursday in July, Kovač was again the attending physician: he said that he'd be releasing Danilo in a couple of days, and that Danilo was doing fairly well.

Two days later, I came back yet again; I found Danilo in the so-called activity room: 'Lidia, where are you always going off to?'

'Danilo, what can I bring you tomorrow?'

'Listen, Lidia, I'm forever dreaming that I'm crying.'

'And what of it, Danilo? Other people have dreams, too.'

'But I feel sick afterwards, Lidia.'

'Other people also feel sick, Danilo. Don't make such a huge drama out of everything.'

'How beautiful you are, Lida, like Marina and like Mira!'

'Don't talk nonsense. You're always faking, and there's nothing wrong with you. You're pretending.'

Danilo takes my cigarette, and asks: 'Give me one smoke.' With his eyes gaping, he puffs on my cigarette.

'I can't, Lidia, I can't stand it any longer. I dream constantly that I'm dying and I'm constantly crying, Lidia, and I dream that I'm crying. And see this guy here?' (He points at a dark-skinned boy.) 'He never quits yelling at me and shoving me as I walk down the hall. I can't do this ...'

I looked at his sweaty, pale face; I thought, my God, he looks so much like Marina, even then (now, as I was talking), when a droplet (a little bubble) of spit had become stuck on the middle part of his lower lip, and as he spoke the little bubble moved just a touch, as if it were a bit of paper. I asked him: 'Danilo, do you want a little juice, no, don't hold the straw like that, here you go ... oh God, you're so clumsy, now you've got it all over yourself,' staring at Marina's saliva droplet-bubble, on account of which I felt like I could slap both of them into the middle of next week.

XXIX

A FINGER IN THE EYE

They called at ten in the morning from Palmotićeva; no one had witnessed anything, no one knew anything, Danilo had been dead the whole blessed night. The bathtub was full of blood – when the tall blonde nurse arrived, the one who sits in the registration office, on the left side when you go into the clinic – he'd cut the veins on one arm only, his left, and the door to the bathroom was jammed shut with nothing but a thin wooden chair from the dining room. Danilo had gone into the bathroom and sliced open his veins, put the rickety chair in place, sat down on the tub, and waited; seriously, he waited, earnestly, for someone to show up and stop his bleeding. The doctor on duty was asleep; the night-nurses were crocheting. When I got there, Danilo was already in some other unit, where they were cutting him up for various and sundry fucked-up reasons; the tall blonde nurse led me upstairs, opened the door to the bathroom, pointed out the blood to me and said: 'I need to get this wrapped up, on account of my other patients.' They didn't ask me any questions and I never saw Danilo again; three of them alternated babbling to me about the regulations; the director was on vacation, as was Kovač. The tall blonde nurse stated: 'I'm sure you can see.' Another nurse said, blinking her early-morning make-up-coated vulgar little eyes: 'We don't keep people tied up here … ' And the doctor, fresh from sleep and in good humour, I mean, why should a corpse spoil his day, he said, picking up a little cup of coffee from the desk (it was the director's office): 'You know, there wasn't anything here that was … ' But he never finished, that part about how he was sorry and what not – I broke his glasses, with my fists, and then I hurled myself at the tall blonde nurse, who was holding the papers in her hands, and I succeeded in tearing out a little of her hair, and I landed a few slaps on her, but that's all, nothing more – may Jaglika's God, Danilo, and Jaglika herself forgive me. I was rash; the three of them got their shit together at the last minute: they held onto my arms with full doctor-nurse strength; the doctor talked some bullshit about hysteria, the tall blonde nurse said through clenched teeth 'She's so crazy,' the other nurse left to get a needleful of something, and when she returned with the beneficent injection for me, I was already on the way out, down in the lobby the blonde nurse had received a big wad of spit right in the middle of her face, so that she was blind for a moment, and the doctor'd received a kick between his legs, not particularly forceful, yet effective.

If I'd only had a bomb. I know where I would have placed it, with no malice in my heart, as though I were carrying out a holy obligation, calmly; what I mean is, cold-bloodedly. And if I had a second bomb, and another beyond that … I wouldn't be at a loss, in any sense of the word. I'd know where to put them all, there's no pathos at play here, and it's also not futile (I have no way of obtaining bombs), or another squall of pointless anger – nothing of the sort, here under the watchful eye of Jaglika's God, or anyway with his blessing. As for bombs, I could get them from Italy via Marina and the Red Brigade, no joke, and first I'd wrap the fuse around Marina's head with the blessing of Jaglika's God. Marina had kicked off this whole show.

Marina arrived exactly twenty-four hours after I'd informed her of Danilo's death. She came with her husband. I was standing on the balcony when I caught sight of them getting out of a taxi: she looked altogether decorous, and he looked like he always does: and that means he had no look at all; he took her by the arm as they crossed the street; then they disappeared into the doorway; when I opened our door, they were just getting out of the lift – those few steps from the lift to the apartment. Marina, Danilo's mother and my own, came slowly, slowly, looking as though she were going to faint at least ten times; I knew it was theatre, Marina's famous theatre with its sophisticated and precise pantomime techniques. Her husband had been black-haired, grey, and black-haired again; and just for a moment it seemed to me that a sudden blush had hit his cheeks: he found this unpleasant. But then when I got a better look at him: I saw an insolent and calm and fat individual; satisfied with his well-tied black tie, satisfied with my mother's cornflow-er-blue blinking eyes, satisfied with his role in her theatre, from the beginning, and now here on Svetosavska Street, too. Then, Marina, marching in, asked: 'Where is he … Where is he?'

'Who, Mama?' I managed to get out.

'Where did it happen, and why did you permit the autopsy?'

'I didn't. It was already all done by the time they called me.'

'Why didn't you call me right away, Lidia? And who were you expecting anyway?'

'Mother, I can't. I can't tell you anything till this guy leaves …'

Marina's husband obediently stepped outside, obediently and quickly, with an expression of superiority and scorn, which is totally typical of him, aside from its being typical for the faces of all inspectors, investigators past, present, and future; he left us for Jaglika's room, not forgetting to slam the door, however;

what a boor! And immediately after that he made several loud noises with his feet. What, was he clicking his heels or something? Saluting?

Then I told her as much as I knew, what they had told me, what I had assumed, ever since the day he'd gone off to Palmotićeva Street. Marina protested, turned her head toward the window, refused to look at me while I was speaking to her; she pressed her lips together in anger, into a thin furious line; and at that point we were both silent for a while, but what needed to be said at that point, anyway? Marina's husband was saluting again in Jaglika's bedroom. All at once her rage burst forth (I suppose it was more than anything because some portion of her theatrical technique had failed her): and with unfathomable derision, fury, saluting could be heard again from Jaglika's room, which now I could understand only as their joint training, I don't believe that it was by chance, and she screamed: 'Why didn't you do something... How could you abandon him' She was waving her hands right in front of my face, and drawing dangerously close to me, so much so that her face called forth all the hatred, every iota of it, that I'd been storing up, nurturing, for years, for my whole life actually... 'What, how could I have, what should I have done?' This was muffled by my intense desire to bust open her fucking mechanical-theatrical head, and smash that face on which for as long as I can recall there was never anything save powder and lipstick.

'Why'd you send him to the hospital?'

'He would've killed himself here, too.'

'But you could've... Didn't you notice anything?'

'Listen, Danilo killed himself; they found him yesterday morning in the bathroom; he had wedged the door shut, Danilo wanted to kill himself, Danilo did kill himself, do you understand he didn't get run over by a car, which you would have preferred, and that is probably the only normal thing, the one normal thing he did, and now stop blinking, stop blinking, stop your blinking… '

She pulled back as if to hit me, but in that instant the thud of footsteps could again be heard in Jaglika's room, like code, a message, what in the… and right away Marina, as if by secret sign, lowered her hand and said in a placating voice: 'If you'd called me, I would have come …'

At that moment (at every moment, in fact, I was capable of killing her) I shook her by the collar of that expensive dress of hers (Marina arrived from Milan all done up: with make-up, sweet blinking little eyes, pearls around her neck). She pushed me aside with one hand, but this wasn't a question of physical strength but rather her actual power over me; she shattered, with the movement of a god and while she was full of loathing, the whole of my lethal rage. Jaglika also possessed this kind of power, and in equal measure. Then she announced, she just declared:

'It's your fault. You sent him to the hospital.'

'Fine, Mother. At least now we both have a soul on our consciences. You have Dad, and I have Danilo. It's just a shame that it's not the other way around. It should be the other way around – the two of them should still be alive …'

'You animal! It was what he himself wanted. He was responsible for landing himself in prison because he wouldn't be quiet. He was guilty, do you understand, you *animaaal*, he himself, get it through your head, no one could have stopped him, he hanged himself, d'you *underststaaand*!?'

'Himself! But it was you, Mother, who sent him. You. How is it possible for you not to know, and those convulsing legs of his – that grand decision was yours, Mother.'

The stamping of feet in Jaglika's room stopped completely, and Marina's husband came out to hold Marina – who had fainted again. I rushed outside. I needed air; it stunk in the house, unbearably. When I returned later that evening, I found them in the midst of some confidential discussion. I didn't enter the room; I had no desire to see my Mother freshly powdered and refreshed after a good nap. Later I heard the opening and shutting of the outside door as they went out to dinner.

Danilo was buried the following day. The hospital delivered him in a closed sheet-metal casket, and no one knew what was inside, what parts of Danilo. Danilo's girlfriend Mira didn't come. She came the next day, after the burial. When they were shovelling out the soil, and as they started lowering the casket in, especially by that point, Marko Eyepiece, who had been standing on the edge of the hole the whole time, really close, with all those bags of his, began gushing tears, and he took off his glasses and smeared snot all over his face, and almost fell into the grave. He looked at me, and at Marina, and he rushed towards the exit without looking back. I never saw him again.

Marina and her husband left by train that same day; with her eyes blinking, she stated that it would be intolerable to spend another moment with me and all my suffocating hatred, that she already had enough torment in her life, and that she'd rather go back on foot than spend another night in Svetosavska Street.

Marina stubbornly cultivated a deep sense of compassion for her own person, like, by the way, all lower-order animals, and she was scared and undeviating in asking about the causes. And of course she believed that in both cases it was insanity, like father like son, and she, ah – she bore none of the blame for it. Both my father and

Danilo lost their own minds, by themselves, and ceased to be; they pulled the blanket up over their own heads. That's what Marina thought. She clung firmly to her mind and her life, with her legs arms breasts husbands and whatever else existed and came her way. She departed with a knot of fear and a lot of luggage, and I do not know where she will hide it, what corner she'll kick it into and how she'll prevail over it. As she was putting on her face in the bathroom before departing, she said this about my father, the same thing, yet again: 'What do you want to hear Lidia he wanted it; it was his choice.' As for Danilo, she might manage to find a more successful way of consoling herself, deluding herself. 'Lidia let him go, and if I'd been here it would not have happened; nothing would have happened.' Jaglika used to talk, for instance, about how my father abandoned his Marina, and how he never, ever should have dared to do that.

Actually, Marina fled, heedlessly, just as Marko Eyepiece had done. And if she could have, she would surely have put up a headstone for Danilo and for my father, two for the price of one, double or nothing, like they did in 1823 in Chelsea for the man Griffiths, who'd committed suicide, if she could have, and if the same penalties were in force today for suicide as back then.

The next day, I tried briefly to imitate Marina a little. I painstakingly dressed up, put on make-up in the bathroom, while loudly trying to say Marina's words: 'he himself wanted it, it was his choice.' Plain and simple, for a moment I was Marina, but it didn't work. It didn't work at all. I smashed the mirror, and then locked Jaglika's room up and transferred my things to Danilo's room. I was incapable of doing the simplest things that both Milena and Marina could so easily do: when you're cold, get dressed, when you're hungry, eat something, when your eyes open, get out of bed; neither one of them, however, grasped the complexity and nausea connected with the most ordinary actions: moving one's leg when your foot falls asleep, taking aspirin for a toothache, getting out of bed in general, or lying in bed in general, and so on, on down the line. Marina – a biological fact in my life, devoid of any greater meaning for the two of us, maternal warmth, I tried that with Milena; and now, you have to admit, any further attempt, at least a willing one, would be superfluous, to play the role of Marina or Milena in front of the mirror.

Instead of these stupid identity games, it could be like this: I simply imagine that I'm, let's say, a bank clerk, and to the first man who turns up at my counter, I say, bankerly-cordially: 'Here you are, sir,' and subsequently I tell my colleague to the left, the one with the big boobs, when the gentleman leaves: 'Damn, isn't that man fine. So smooth. I recognize him from earlier and he's been a customer here for ages … ' and she will start trembling on the peak of her left breast where the Olympic Games symbol is and sighing as if she were rapidly expiring, perishing like a big old dog; or, for instance, I imagine that I'm a conductor in the municipal mass transit system and that every day I smell people's stink and my own, too, and it's something that doesn't bother me in the least. On the contrary. I punch tickets and dream that I'm marrying the mayor, or even the district commissioner, *ooooh*, that would be so classy.

In lieu of all that, I turn up out of breath at work, my work, winded by the fog, the bus, other people running in front of and behind me, next to me and across my path. But where does fog come from in August? I confabulated it. Ran smack into my boss, or his double. Both of them, as a matter of fact. When they caught sight of me at the door, one of them, or both of them simultaneously, said: 'But you don't have to come in your brother he …'

'My brother killed himself. Did you know that a thousand people kill themselves every day?'

'Where? Here, in our country?' They stared at each other in astonishment.

'Well, *nooo*. A thousand people per day across the surface of the earth.'

'Okay, okay … You came to work?'

'I came to fix your eyes (for both of you, I thought to myself) in case your operation didn't take.'

The boss eyed me and my outstretched arms for a moment, flabbergasted, and then he remembered that my brother was one of the thousand, and he quite reasonably thought that I had, just for a moment, lost my mind in all the agitation. And even more reasonably (but therefore no less stupidly) he said: 'It would be better for you to go on home, Lidia, and rest up. And you're entitled to five more days …'

Seeing me beaming, however, and on the verge of hysterical laughter (so it seemed to him), he reached timorously for the telephone, but he'd had the wherewithal to make known as a warning and as an assertion: 'You aren't well.'

'I feel wonderful. I just want to put your eyes back in, carefully, with the tips of my fingers. It'll just take a minute.' I had lifted my hands into the air again. The boss's double was already dialling the telephone. Whom was he calling? The city ambulance service? I went outside, with the realization that Danilo was right, and that I had quarrelled needlessly with him that day. It was all the same if my boss had Graves' disease or just looked that way. Pressing his eyeballs back, slowly, tenderly, or just saying so to him, was the same thing, utterly the same. The eyes of both my boss and his double returned to their proper spots.

A Story from Childhood

I think this happened, that it used to happen when I was six or seven, but certainly no older than that; there were ten of us children, but there were actually more of us, although I'm saying it this way now, because it seems right: ten; the reason for this numerical mix-up: it's more in the realm of logic (various theories of probability show, naturally, varying possibilities; sometimes numerical values are distinct, that is to say, calculable, but sometimes they just aren't), and corresponding to it, I mean, in harmony with this logical 'confusion' like a little flash of reflected light, or, to put it simply, and better: like a really small shadow this 'confusion' appears in my 'memory'. With that said: something that does not exist is something that is also non-existent, with the same frequency of occurrence and without the possibility of numerical calculability. Thus it follows: we hopped a ride on the outside of a tram; it was racing at an incalculable rate past posts, telephone poles, and the whole breadth of the Kalemegdan hill; and behind me, adhering to me (that's the smallest distance that exists) was a puny little man with glasses and a beret. Before me was a female being in a jumper; I had jammed my head into her shoulder (fear) and my fingers into her jumper (it had a loose weave). I was scared that I would fall, since I'd never ridden on the outside of a tram before. Back then the tracks ran so close to the branches of the trees that every ride-hopping was the most improbable of accomplishments; in every curve I had to turn my head, to nestle it against the car, just so that it didn't get plucked off by some passing branch or pole. Everybody on the tram was a child, although they looked like adults. By the last stop I was drenched with fear, the tram slowed to a stop, of course; and the female wearing a jumper, that loosely woven jumper, was, as I could tell when I dismounted, a little girl from the building next to mine, whom I'd never seen wearing a jumper before. Jaglika was waiting at the station, and the first thing she did when I got off was to slap me three times, and then she jerked me along for ten minutes, by both ears, with both of her hands – for a whole year my ears were red and puffy. When we reached Svetosavska, and got near our door, she said she was going to tell Marina everything, and Marina was going to beat the daylights out of me so I'd remember what's allowed and what's possible and, for God's sake, what is just not ever allowed and not at all possible … "

A Death in the Neighbourhood:

On the Work of Biljana Jovanović

The novel you have before you is strong medicine. It depicts a young person's attempt to 'invent her childhood' and 'liberate her memory' while she negotiates a bohemian, urban existence in Yugoslavia in the 1970s; it is more than graphic, and painful, and awkward at times: it is a tale of catastrophe, really and truly, annihilating catastrophe – but also of great courage. The narrator, Lidia, is rigorously probing her often wretched memories of neglect from childhood, even as she tries vigorously to navigate humanely her complicated living situation in Zemun (in greater Belgrade) in the apartment of her long-gone mother, which she shares with her dying grandmother and her suicidal brother. But the author also shows great courage here. That is why *Dogs and Others* is the single most effective introduction to the oeuvre of Biljana Jovanović (1953–1996), an important Serbian novelist and dramatist who is almost completely unknown outside of her home country.

Jovanović herself died of cancer in 1996; she was only forty-three years old. In the novel at hand, a different death provides the climax of the story: the protagonist's brother commits suicide in the shattering resolution of the dysfunctional relationships and emotional drift of the various characters. And, as Jovanović herself noted in interviews, the country of Yugoslavia, which was the setting of her works, in all their concrete, cacophonous, rebellious, and tender glory, also died in the 1990s. It felt like the end of the world, to paraphrase the author; and it cut the lives of her generation in half: between the past, memory, and nostalgia, and, in the other direction, war and nothing.

Who was Biljana Jovanović?

Biljana Jovanović (1953–1996) was a Serbian intellectual who wrote in almost all major genres; she published four plays, three novels, two collections of letters, and one anthology of poetry, as well as a sizable number of non-fiction pieces, mostly connected to her political activism. The popularity of her writings, especially her first two novels, has positioned her as a perennially beloved figure on today's Serbian literary scene, even as her actual profile evolves from being a popular counter-cultural figure (even an author of 'cult classics') to more of a 'writer's writer'. As widely known, and rightfully admired, as she is among intellectuals and activists for her work in civil society, she was also a talented and courageous writer of fiction and drama.

Jovanović's family had Montenegrin roots and, although she was born in Belgrade, she maintained active ties to that part of Yugoslavia. Her father, Batrić Jovanović, was a military official and political functionary in Tito's Yugoslavia; her mother was Olga Ćetković, a journalist; both parents had been Partisans during the Second World War. The youngest of three children, Jovanović enrolled at the University of Belgrade in 1972 and studied philosophy. She was an early and active member of a large number of important human rights groups in Yugoslavia, beginning in 1982. These groups were concerned with issues from the death penalty to the environment, and from artistic freedom to feminism. Two of her most famous engagements were with the Belgrade Circle and the Civil Opposition Movement, both in the 1990s, when she had to add anti-war activism to her earlier engagements for pluralism and justice. She was an organizer and participant in a number of major anti-war campaigns and events, and she helped found a 'flying' (underground) workshop (or university) in 1992.

While working as an editor and proof-reader, including at the prestigious journal *Književne novine*, she wrote three novels. These appeared in print in short order: *Pada Avala* (1978), *Psi i ostali* (1980), and *Duša, jedinica moja* (1984). Her writing for the stage began in the 1970s and lasted through until the end of her life. Unfortunately, very little of her work is available in English, although a few excerpts can be found online , and there are two book-length items (though no novels) in the bibliography at the end of this essay. Since 2006 there has been a major literary prize in Serbia that is named for her, awarded by the prestigious *Srpsko književno društvo* (The Serbian Literary Society), and there have recently been conferences, retrospectives, a noticeable increase in scholarly attention about her writing, and reprints of her works.

Whether Jovanović is, in the final analysis, considered primarily a pioneer of 'jeans prose', a feminist, a vulnerable and extremely sensitive but also powerful witness to nationalist, authoritarian, and patriarchal anachronisms, a 'rebel with a cause' (as the title of the major anthology released on the 20th anniversary of her death reads in translation), an avant-garde experimentalist, a chronicler of the Yugoslav socialist experiment, or all of the above, her prose is both descriptive and normative in new ways. Jovanović was growing up as the unsolved contradictions of the reign of Josip Broz Tito and the League of Communists were emerging from the shadows of the anti-fascist moment and the Cold War. In the opinion of this translator and historian, she is remarkable not only for her civil courage, but also for her intellectual perspectives and her rich and bracing writing.

About This Book

This novel is a quest. It is built of a spare plot much enriched by flashbacks and letters of various types. The glue that holds its pieces together is a particular epistemology, more or less articulated in various barely-disguised authorial interventions sprinkled through-out the text(s), along with a pell-mell, 'take-no-prisoners' style of narration that is well suited to capture the tumult of Lidia's life and surroundings. And the whole thing ends up feeling like an acid bath. Everything is stripped of its façade or patina, all paradoxes melt away, and we are left with excruciating truths about power and loss. Only pain survives this book. We can hope our vision is a bit sharper, too.

This is Jovanović's second novel, and it is, to say the least, highly unconventional. 'Avant-garde' is a better characterization. It is set in Belgrade in the 1960s and 1970s, and through a fragmentary narrative replete with intertextuality and interior monologues ('stream of consciousness'), it tracks the life of a young woman named Lidia. The lives depicted in the novel are probably more 'counter-cultural' than 'bohemian' per se, but above all they are modern, and urban. Lidia's family life is pulling apart at the seams due to old age, disability, mental illness, drug use, and suicide; her very personhood is also bedevilled by memories of an abusive childhood that are still very much alive, but also by sexism, sexual harassment, and sexual assault in her adult world. Lidia is raped by her psychiatrist and sexually assaulted by her boss; her love Milena is assaulted by her dentist and, in turn, sexually assaults an intellectually disabled patient in her care.

A kind of frame tale is set up in the first chapter, with the narrator and her grandmother, Jaglika, positioned to complete each other's stories about the history of the family. The narrative is constantly disrupted by the unexpected appearance and disappearance of characters, by the insertion of a group of detailed and disturbing letters from an anonymous neighbour, by often unmoored 'Images from Childhood', and by frequent use of words such as 'the others', 'the rest', 'all', and 'everything'. In addition, the author takes an experimental approach to punctuation, spelling, paragraph structure, attribution, epigrams, chapter titles, and, of course, chronology, so that the reader, breathless and sometimes even partially blind, is hurtled through the story and plunged into situations awash in carefully calibrated amounts of what seem to be random detail and suffering. The novel works hard, and it works the reader hard, but with great effect.

The death of Lidia's brother, mirroring that of her father, casts her progress in trying to understand her world into doubt, if not into a nose-dive. The novel even closes with a reference back to the cryptic preface of the book, underscoring the bleakness of the burden of self-assertion and social adaptation.

An Appreciation

Translators read books multiple times, and they do so very carefully. Your translator for this volume also happens to be a historian of the twentieth-century Balkans, and, while that is far from a guarantee of good taste or good sense, it might mean that the things I appreciate about this novel, or wish to underscore in some way or another because they 'worked for me', are singular enough to provide new food for thought.

For this reader, some of the most memorable scenes in the book involve Jaglika, the *baba* (grandmother) of Lidia and Danilo. She is a kind of unifying or intersecting axis across multiple generations and ethnicities, and parts of her life story also appear in other places in Jovanovic's fiction. The apartment in which most of the family lives, although only partially described, is the site of a wondrous number of comings and goings; it's located in an out-of-the-way part of greater Belgrade, but the number of visitors, all seeking different things – from trysts to funeral visitations to porn screenings to jobs and lodgings and beyond – make it a microcosm of the urban world. The way Jaglika's physical decline is charted, and the interactions of her family members in its shadow, is thought-provoking and disarmingly unconventional. The impact of the two startling incidents in Belgrade trams or buses, one involving Lidia and the other her brother, endures in a cinematic style, long after reading. While the tragedy with Danilo is doubtlessly the dramatic turning point of the novel, Chapter 22 seems to realize the potential of much of the book with the brutal clarity and expanse of its elaborations; the chapter is a calling card for the entire work, ready to be anthologized.

Some of the appeal of this novel to historians, or to people from the western Balkans, might stem from the reality of local life that populates the narrative. These 'assemblages' of Yugoslav products and practices range from cafe fare (*tulumba, krempita, boza*) to UNICEF greeting cards and specific consumer items such as rice, soap, and bleach, and from summer vacations in Italy and Istria and reading circles to Sunday family strolls along Knez Mihailova in downtown Belgrade. We are also on the edge of the world of books and literature and universities when we are in Lidia's world: there are libraries, class notes and hand-outs, and references to Dostoyevsky, Balzac, Castaneda, Dewey, Bergson, Schopenhauer, and Mann.

The relationship between Lidia and Milena, in evidence from Chapter 7 till its demise in Chapter 23, is tracked fearlessly from attraction through sex to toxic arguments. Some of these passages are startlingly evocative in the service of emotional and physical connections; some of them are flat-out beautiful, in a very modern way.

Conclusion

This book takes us from a scene in which a mother, flashing 'encoded family glances' and telling a grandmother 'This child's never going to stop lying. We're taking her to the doctor' to a daughter longing for the chance to acquire explosives from the Red Brigades in Italy and blow her mother's head off. That's what was meant back in the opening sentence of this essay about 'strong medicine'. It is a novel, one could say, of backbiting and recrimination that gives way to excavations of mental and physical abuse and sexual violence and more, and ends in full-blown social critique.

In style and impact, perhaps an analogue to Dogs and Others might be found in the compelling novels of the British Nobel

Prize laureate Doris Lessing (1919–2013) or the Quebecois novelist Hubert Aquin (1929–1977); many other comparisons to writers outside the South Slavic sphere are doubtless possible. In addition, Yugoslavia never lacked for hard-hitting and inventive authors, in any epoch. But within Serbian literature, it would be hard to find, even at the late date of her writing within the trajectory of Yugoslavia, a writer who carried a bigger set of thematic and political concerns into innovative texts. And, in terms of women writers, Jovanović arguably joins Judita Šalgo (1941–1996) and Milica Mićić-Dimovska (1947–2013) in the vanguard of challenging and accomplished artists.

As this translation goes to press, the #MeToo movement is over a year old and is still growing in social and political importance. It is impossible not to notice the amount of sexual harassment, abuse, and assault in this novel, which itself is 38-year-old evidence in a millennia-old struggle for voice and redress. It is not too much to ask that we stay open to questions asked by older novels. And this is true also about the reception accorded to innovative or transgressive writings. Therefore, over time, it is quite possible that the study of Jovanović's novels and their real-life trajectories will tell us a lot about what life was like in socialist Yugoslavia and what went wrong with Titoism.

Bibliography

Works by Biljana Jovanović

Poems:

Čuvar: pesme (Belgrade: Književna omladina Srbije, 1977)

Novels:

Pada Avala (Belgrade: Prosveta, 1978 and several later editions [1981, 2006, 2016])

Psi i ostali (Belgrade: Prosveta, 1980 and several later editions [2007 and 2016])

Duša, jedinica moja (Belgrade: BIGZ, 1984)

Plays:

Ulrike Majnhof (1976)

Leti u goru kao ptica (1982)

Centralni zatvor (1990)

Soba na Bosforu (1994)

Nonfiction:

Vjetar ide na jug i obrće se na sjever (with Rada Iveković, Maruša Kreše, and Radmila Lazić). Belgrade: Radio B92, 1994.

Non omnis moriar: prepiska (correspondence with Josip Osti). Ljubljana: Vodnikova domačija, 1996.

Works about Biljana Jovanović

Dojčinović, Biljana. "Representations of Body in Contemporary Women's Writing in Serbia." Conference paper. Unpublished.

————. "Telo kao globalizovano odelo: konstrukt telesnosti i tekstualnosti u romanu *Mango* Ljubice Arsić." In Agnieszka Matusiak, et al, eds., *Wielkie tematy kultury w literaturach słowiańskich* (Wroclaw: Wydawnictwo Uniwerzytetu Wrocławskiego, 2011), pp. 145-150

Đurovic, Jovana. "Čitati Biljanu Jovanović danas." Conference paper. Available at academia.edu/9588946/Čitati_Biljanu_Jovanović_danas

Lazić, Radmila, and Urošević, Miloš, eds. *Biljana Jovanović: Buntovnica s razlogom*. Belgrade: Žene u crnom/Women in Black, 2016.

Lukic, Jasmina. "Protiv svih zabrana." *ProFemina*, no. 7 (Summer 1996), pp. 126-134.

Pavićević, Borka. "Glava u torbi: Duša jedinica moja." *Danas*. 11 March 2016.

Slapšak, Svetlana. "*Soba na Bosforu* Biljane Jovanović." *ProFemina*, no. 7 (Summer 1996), pp. 144-145.

Existing Translations

Jovanović, Biljana; Iveković, Rada; Kreše, Maruša; and Lazić, Radmila. *Briefe von Frauen über Krieg und Nationalismus*. Translated by Barbara Antkowiak and Marina Einspieler. Frankfurt: Suhrkamp, 1993.

Jovanović, Biljana. *Maison centrale: jeu dramatique en deux actes; Une chambre sur le Bosphore: jeu dramatique en neuf scènes, avec neuf fenêtres*. Translated by Mireille Robin. Paris: Éditions L'Espace d'un instant, 2010.

The Translator

JOHN K. COX is a professor of East European History at North Dakota State University in Fargo. He earned his PhD from Indiana University-Bloomington in 1995 and specializes in modern Balkan and Central European intellectual history. His translations include works by Danilo Kiš, Miklós Radnóti, Muharem Bazdulj, Ivan Cankar, Radomir Konstantinović, Stefan Heym, Goran Petrović, Ismail Kadare, Ajla Terzić, and Vesna Perić. He is currently translating other works by Biljana Jovanović as well as novels by Dragana Kršenković Brković and Erzsébet Galgóczi.

Lightning Source UK Ltd.
Milton Keynes UK
UKHW021216171118
332499UK00005B/188/P